Inappropriate Behaviour

Inappropriate Behaviour

IRENE MOCK

Porcépic Books
an imprint of

BEACH HOLME PUBLISHING
VANCOUVER

The publisher gratefully acknowledges financial assistance from the
Canada Council and the BC Ministry of Small Business, Tourism
and Culture. This is a Porcépic book.

Edited by Joy Gugeler
Text design by Carolyn Stewart
Cover design and illustration by Doug Jones
Printed and bound in Canada by Webcom Ltd.

CANADIAN CATALOGUING IN PUBLICATION DATA

Mock, Irene, 1949–
Inappropriate behaviour

"A Porcépic Book."
ISBN 0-88878-374-4

1. Women–Fiction. I. Title. II. Series.
PS8576.O24I52 1997   C813'.54   C96-901060-5
PR9199.3.M58I52 1997

BEACH HOLME PUBLISHING
#226–2040 WEST 12TH AVENUE
VANCOUVER, BC   V6J 2G2   CANADA

For David, Anna and Paul

Acknowledgements

The following stories (some in earlier forms and with different titles) were previously published:

"What We Have" and "Satellite Worlds" in *Grain*
"A Small Ceremony" in *Matrix*
"Neapolitan" in *Queen's Quarterly*
"Inappropriate Behaviour" in *The Capilano Review* (nominated for the 1996 Journey Prize)
"To Be Young, To Be Beautiful" in *Island*
"Rapture" in *The Fiddlehead*
"Lovers and Other Strangers" in *Descant*
"Fire" in *The Canadian Forum*

The author is grateful to her family for their unfailing support and to Joy Gugeler for her sharp editorial eye. She also wishes to thank those who commented on earlier versions of these stories, especially Verna Relkoff.

If I tell you a story about terrible things happening, I can surround it with language, I can give it a body that is much more palatable than the events themselves were and you can carry it in your memory as a warning, or as a caution of some kind. And I who tell it can comprehend it that much more. I mean, telling is always, in all of its incarnations an act of optimism.

— RICHARD FORD

Contents

Firstborn

What We Have
A Small Ceremony
Red Beads

What We Have

Our beginnings are utterly mysterious—why are we born?
Why when and as we are?

ON NIGHTS WHEN SHE COULDN'T SLEEP Julie would
go into the room meant for the baby. She would look
at the bassinet, the tiny clothes, the stuffed animals. Then
she would come back to bed.

"Michael?" She touched his shoulder. "Michael,
keep thinking about the baby."

He struggled to wake up, put an arm aroun'
"Jules—honey, you know these things happen."

Yes, she thought, but there's got to be a r

two glasses of wine on Michael's birthday. Or maybe the week she was sick with flu in her first trimester? Or perhaps something larger. Some lack of faith?

"Michael," she said. "Promise me you won't tell anyone what's wrong with the baby."

She touched his hair but he frowned and pushed her hand away. "You know, it's not easy for me either."

She shuddered, drawing her hand over her swollen belly. *Inside my body, my husband and I have created an abomination*. In primitive times such a baby wouldn't be allowed to live. Probably the mother, she thought, wouldn't be allowed to live either. Maybe her mate would have killed her. Even twins—normal twins—were put to death because only animals had litters, so the mother must have mated with an animal. Did Michael know what *they'd* created? Did he have any idea?

"Michael," she said, "will you promise me please?"

It hadn't moved for several days, maybe longer. But the baby had never moved much anyway. She didn't want to bother Michael so she distracted herself, painting the baby's room, going to all the fitness and pre-natal classes. Still, when her father had greeted her over the phone with his proud, "Hello, Mother!" she had to protest. "Dad, please don't say that. I'm not a mother yet."

Why didn't she tell Michael then that she felt something was wrong with the baby? She knew all the things that could go wrong. It had annoyed her when friends said how well it was growing. When some would pat her belly and laugh. And wasn't it just like the doctor, when he couldn't find the heartbeat—three days ago at her regular eighth month check-up—to jiggle her belly, to say jokingly to the baby, "Wake up!" Finally, though, he'd given up, sent her for an ultrasound. . . .

The baby had been her idea. When they were talking about having it in their second year together, Michael was uncertain. Once she became pregnant, he began buying her vitamin supplements, talking about the trips the three of them would take, starting a special bank account for the baby. He built a little table and chair set for her thirty-fourth birthday.

Put the baby things away, people told them. Put them away. There'll be another time.

But whenever she went out Julie noticed how cautiously they approached, their trapped look as they avoided her big belly.

"You'll try again. Won't you?" they'd say.

SHE COLLECTED THE CLOTHES in a bag. Bending over, annoyed at her big belly, she helped Michael dismantle the crib. They put away the stroller, the Snugli, the bassinet. She felt him keep his distance, afraid, even accidentally, to touch.

Just as they were finishing, Bob and Andrea stopped by. She and Andrea had gone through their pregnancies together discussing everything from her Cheerios and ice cream, Julie's pickled herring and cheese, to birth positions ("On my side," Andrea joked, "like a voluptuous Rubenesque painting.")

Once she'd asked how Andrea felt about bringing a child into today's world and she said, "Not hopeful. But even five or six years with a child would be better than nothing."

Not long ago, at a party, she'd overheard a man say, "You know when a war's going to break out because right before it happens everyone gets pregnant. Something to do with survival of the species . . . ."

She looked at Andrea's big belly now, then down at her own. "Is there anything more you need for the baby?" she asked. "Please. Go upstairs and see."

When Andrea came back, her hands hung empty at her side. "We still need a bassinet, but . . . are you sure?"

The bassinet. It was one of those silly things—white, with pink and blue cats. Julie had found it at a garage sale. She and Michael had sung as they brought the bassinet into the living room, falling exhausted on the couch. Andrea had complimented them on their good fortune. "I've gone to all the garage sales and haven't come across one bassinet yet. You must be lucky."

"My, what ridiculous looking cats!" Andrea laughed nervously now, as Michael helped Bob carry the bassinet downstairs. "It's bad enough you can't get anything for a baby that isn't pink or blue. But cats with *both* colours?"

Julie waved as Bob and Andrea pulled away. When they were gone, Michael turned to her and they held each other in the driveway. "I love your hair, Jules," he whispered, stroking the fine red strands that fell to her shoulders.

A WEEK PASSED. It had been four weeks since the doctor last heard the heartbeat. He was concerned. "If another week goes by you could risk spontaneous haemorrhages which can be fatal, but," he tried, seeking to reassure them, "there's still only a small chance of this occurring."

She nodded. How calm, professional he was. She could feel her eyes glaze over. "What would you recommend?"

The doctor appeared thoughtful. "You could have it out right away, of course."

A C-section. Michael agreed. "They're quite common, honey. Lots of women have them."

She nodded again, but she felt cheated. "Actually, I'd prefer not to." Couldn't she have *anything*?

The doctor looked down. "Well dear, it could be difficult. Without a head . . . ."

"Without a head?" *Why say that*? She glanced at Michael, then back at the doctor.

"What I mean is, since the head's not fully developed. . . . Since it may not dilate the cervix . . . ." The doctor shrugged to indicate how useless it was to explain. "Well Julie, you're a nurse, I'm sure you understand."

"Why not get a C-section?" Michael argued. "Surely you don't need to carry it any longer."

"It. Why does everyone make it seem as if I'm walking around with a rotten vegetable," she said, "a turnip or cabbage."

He put his arm around her. "Don't you just want to get the baby out and be done with this?"

No. She did not. Though just why she couldn't explain. She took Michael's hand from her shoulder and pressed it between her own hands which were cold, shaking. *Inside my body, my husband and I created a baby with no head. No brain,* she thought. *Not human.* But the baby

didn't feel that way to her. This baby was her dream.
Even a dream that died, you didn't stop carrying.

She would not have the baby taken from her.

TO DISGUISE HER PREGNANCY, she wrapped herself in
Michael's huge raincoat. She didn't want strangers coo-
ing over her now. She didn't want anyone patting her
belly. Above all, she didn't want to have the baby where
everybody knew her; where all the nurses she worked
with would offer their sympathy, and see the child. She
and Michael had decided on Vancouver. It was well over
five hundred miles away but they had friends there—or
could, if they wanted, remain anonymous. Maybe she
wouldn't need the C-section; a specialist could induce
labour. In case she had any problems with the airline, the
doctor had given her a note: *May travel by air, thirty-four
weeks pregnant, not in labour.*

This was not entirely true. She was over thirty-six
weeks, actually, and women are not supposed to fly in
their last month of pregnancy. She'd started having
irregular contractions the night before. But that morning when the doctor examined her and referred her
to a specialist she had been reassured it would be safe
to fly.

Now she was afraid she might have the baby on the
plane. She didn't want anyone to see it. She wasn't sure
if even she and Michael would want to.

Before they'd decided to go to Vancouver, she'd told
the doctor they planned to look at the baby.

He advised against it. "You never know how you or

your husband will react. And then it will be too late to wish you hadn't."

"But I'm a nurse," she'd said. "I've seen babies like this."

"An *anencephalic?*" He looked at her as if she were crazy. "Usually these babies are miscarried early because the brain is absent or so poorly developed. But," he shrugged, "I'm sure you already know that."

He could have said *anencephalic monster*, that's what the medical books called it. She read in one text, *A sizeable number of cases have been suspected to be environmental: a maternal fever in early pregnancy, pesticides and herbicides, recent potato blights in the United Kingdom.* There was a small photograph in a book by a lay-midwife who wrote, *These babies have, for some reason, disproportionately long arms and legs.* But the baby, who had lived a week, wore a scarf around its head.

"I can always decide at the time, can't I?" she'd told the doctor.

He shrugged. "The decision's yours. But if it were up to me—if you were my daughter—I certainly wouldn't want you to."

She stared at him.

"You know, you might be risking your marriage."

"My marriage?" She looked at Michael and laughed.

"It may affect how you make love. Sometimes it can produce such guilt . . . ."

She sucked in her breath.

"This kind of baby is worse than anything you've seen. Not even nurses like these babies," he said.

HALF PAST MIDNIGHT. The delivery room was dark except for a small lamp in the corner. Julie's doctor—the new one, a specialist—stood bent over the baby and talked to the nurse. Julie couldn't hear what he was saying but when he approached the bed he told her, "I always encourage my patients to see the baby. I think it helps."

Now she and Michael were alone in the delivery room with the baby and nurse.

"Does the baby look human?" Julie asked.

The nurse said, "Yes."

"Are you sure?"

"Yes. Let me show him to you."

There was nothing left to do now but to look. The nurse brought the baby close. She had wrapped him carefully, so that the back of the head was covered by the blanket. The baby had no forehead. He didn't look like a baby at all. "Please," Julie said, "take it away." But just as the nurse turned to go, Julie whispered, "No, please, wait."

"I see an old person," Michael said. Julie cried and looked away.

She reached out and touched the baby's feet. Cold, very cold, but the toes were perfect. Each had a tiny nail, and the skin at the joints was wrinkled.

Then the hands.

Cold, but again, perfectly formed.

Michael took the baby in his arms and held it out to her.

"No," she said, "I can't. I can't."

He turned away with the baby but the nurse said, "Are you sure?"

Michael cradled him in one hand while the other

stroked his small feet. "Julie . . ." he said quietly, holding the child toward her.

THE NEXT MORNING the doctor told her she could go. *It was over.* Leaving the hospital, Michael took her hand and they walked the few short blocks to Queen Elizabeth Park. The sun was hot, the sky clear, and the world suddenly full of people.

"Remember when we first heard the baby's heartbeat in the doctor's office?" he asked.

She looked at him. *Yes.*

"And that time on the patio, when I put my hand on your belly and just at that moment he kicked?"

They stood at a rock wall looking out over the gardens. Below, amidst a profusion of colours, people walked, couples posed in front of flower beds. Young people, old people, men in tuxedos, women in bright wedding gowns.

A Small Ceremony

FOR A WHILE, THE BOX WAS KEPT in Michael's study, not because there wasn't room for it elsewhere but because he always felt it his role to see me through things. It was small, the size of a tea canister, wrapped in brown parcel paper. We sometimes speculated on the contents. We both felt we wanted to shake it, but didn't. Then Michael said he was finding it hard to go into his study with the box there.

"Can't you put it behind a cabinet drawer?" I asked. No, he'd already tried that.

"Behind some books on the shelf?" No, that didn't

work. As long as the box stayed in his study he felt uncomfortable.

Eventually we moved the box to the closet in the spare room, which would have been the baby's. We talked about doing what we'd planned: climb a mountain and have a small ceremony, when we were healthy again, when it was summer, when it was all over.

It is summer now, but we still haven't done it. I've tried to bring up the subject. "It's a lovely day for a hike." Or, "What about climbing Elephant Mountain, going across the bridge?"

Michael is reluctant. And there are additional restrictions now. The mountain has to be further than five miles from where we live. It cannot be within sight, or be where people are likely to go. It must be a place that overlooks a lake, but if it's a very private spot, it can be on a lake and doesn't have to be a mountain top at all. Recently, Michael, who is an avid cross-country skier, has gone so far as to say we shouldn't climb a mountain at all, but rather wait until winter when we can ski up to a remote summit.

"But if we wait until winter," I protest, "Natsumi won't be able to come with us."

"Do you really think she should," he says, "after what she's been through?"

"But she'd want to be there. She's always loved me as her own child."

I was twelve when Natsumi came to New York to live with my family as a nanny. That year kids at school stretched the corners of their eyes and laughed about Japs eating "lice" and "Commies" taking over the world. The year of sirens and air-raid drills—duck and cover—

lying on the floor with hands over our heads so we wouldn't get cut by flying glass when the bomb exploded. People were building bomb shelters and stock-piling powdered milk, canned soup, ammunition.

I remember being very curious. What was her family like? Did people really live in paper houses? Sleep on mats?

One day she showed me a photograph of three girls and pointed to the one in the middle. "Youngest sister, such a pretty one, isn't it?"

The girl she pointed to was the most slender of the three, with a smiling face like the others, but then, in their kimonos, all Japanese women looked alike to me.

"You have such a nice family," she said suddenly.

Confused, I asked, "Isn't yours nice too?"

"Yes, but this world too sad for the human being," she said.

Then she told me about the the loss of her parents and youngest sister. About Hiroshima. About her infant son, who would have been a few years older than I.

"Your family now my family," she said.

This didn't seem quite right to me. She talked differently, for one thing. For another, she was so small. And her sisters wore kimonos.

"No," I answered. "Your family is Japanese."

In my fourth month of pregnancy, during the nightmares, I phoned Natsumi in New York. I kept thinking something was going to happen to the baby. I dreamt I was about to give birth when I heard a loud explosion and everything around me went up in flames.

"We can only believe things turn out right," she told me. "Nobody can ever know." She said she was saving money to come out here, all the way to British

Columbia, to see the baby. That she would not return to Japan until she had.

"Maybe you're right," Michael says. "Maybe she'd want to be here for the ceremony."

I'm not really sure, though, that either one of us is ready. It's almost a truce now, a warding off.

The box stays where it is.

❧

I'M TEMPTED TO REMOVE the box myself. I doubt he'd notice; neither of us goes into the spare room much. The door to that room used to be kept open for ventilation on hot, stuffy nights. But now the door stays closed. Sometimes one of us will go in there and open the window, if it becomes unbearable.

I could move the box, but where would I put it? In the garden? Garage? Certainly not buried in the front lawn.

❧

"OPEN YOUR EYES, silly girl. It won't hurt you," Natsumi would say, "it's only a *hachi*."

Hachi. Japanese for bee. I was in the spare room going through all the baby things again when I heard Natsumi's low voice. I stood in front of the closet door, listening; her voice was so encouraging. I opened the door. On the shelf above the box was an envelope and inside it old photographs of Natsumi and me.

My eye caught the view of the lake from the window. Elephant Mountain. The sun shining; the sky, a radiant blue.

I removed the box and shook it, not sure what I expected to hear. When I didn't hear anything, I shook it again.

Across the street a girl was playing with a ball: throwing it up in the air, then running to catch it. I stood watching her with the box in my hand. If she catches the ball before I count to three, I thought, everything will be all right.

The girl threw the ball high; I counted. As if by some miracle, she caught the ball before I'd finished.

IT WAS SILLY OF ME to tell Michael that I took out the box and shook it. He thinks we may have been cheated, that there's nothing inside.

Even if it were true that what's in the box is *not* what we expect, I hardly think it matters. But Michael is not like me; he needs proof. He still keeps the certificate in a drawer—I don't ask where.

I always expected the worst. At the hospital I watched doctors rush around, attaching tubes and bottles with a frenzied urgency. All this to save lives when every day a new set of insanities is invented to put an end to them.

Michael thinks I look on the gloomy side. "Until a thing happens," he says, "how can you know it will go wrong?" Sardo's Law, he calls it: if you don't think positively, you're not giving yourself a fair chance.

"But bad things do happen," I say. "They happen all the time."

We still can't talk about it.

I'm telling him that I'm phoning Natsumi. We need to do something now.

MICHAEL SEEMS RELIEVED, though he met Natsumi only once, five years ago at our wedding. He's told me *how* close he feels to her. Showing him the photographs of her from my childhood, I think *how* quickly we're no longer children ourselves, but wanting children of our own.

Natsumi looks directly at the camera, shielding her eyes from the sun. I am struck by her petite body, and her thick black hair pinned loosely. She's thirty-three and wears my outgrown clothes from summer camp; shorts, a blue and white T-shirt, and shoes with wedge heels to make her appear taller.

In another, taken when she visits me at camp a year later, Natsumi and I hold hands in front of a rowboat. Although I'm only thirteen, I am a head taller. The man holding the camera is Natsumi's boyfriend. A year later the boyfriend would return to Japan for an arranged marriage to another. Natsumi knew this but, in the photograph, her face is not unhappy, not a bit. The two of them spent the summer travelling through Quebec, crying when it came time to say goodbye.

"Arranged marriages are so stupid!" I said.

Natsumi replied patiently, "This is our way—the Japanese way." It would not be right to interfere with his young bride's happiness.

"But you love each other!" I exclaimed. "It isn't fair."

"This world not always fair," she answered. "Do you think life always fair?"

WE COULD BE GOING on a family outing, an August picnic. The three of us are exuberant. Natsumi looks older, her rich black hair grey now, though she still wears it pinned loosely. She has on a brilliant blue crepe dress that shimmers in the wind and, of course, shoes with wedge heels.

We've come to the park at Sandspit, a forty-five minute drive up the lake from where we live. The sun is hot, the sky clear, but the beach is nearly empty. Several families, probably people who live close by, are clustered together at one end on towels and blankets. Three or four children are building sand castles; other children run in and out of the water. Further on we pass an older couple in folding lawn chairs gazing at the mountains. As we walk along the shore, I stare at the box.

I've been reading about ceremonies: small rituals people perform at burials. I've thought about what we might say.

It has been over a year since we've had the box and I'm pregnant again, but not far along. As we sit on the shore listening to the loons call, I wonder if the child I'm carrying might someday play in this same place. Michael lays the box on the sand gently and looks at me. It's time to unwrap it.

First, the brown parcel paper, slowly removed. Underneath, a cardboard box. I'm disappointed; surely it should have been made of wood, something substantial.

A thin gold ribbon is tied on top. It pulls off easily. Inside, mounds of cotton stuffing stick to tiny white brittle pieces. I keep hoping to see ashes—but there aren't any ashes at all.

"What are these?" I ask.

Natsumi puts her hand into the box and takes some pieces from the bottom.

"Bones," she says, examining them. "My baby's bones must have been like this too."

I look at the tiny white pieces. Then it comes back, what she told me about her son. "There was no time, no time at all," she said. "Everyone was all mixed together, can you imagine? All mixed together in some cans and boxes." There'd been no time to mourn, or to identify. To prevent the spread of disease, the bodies had to be cremated as quickly as possible. Though some boxes were marked with the sites—schools, factories— where the dead were found, their names were unknown.

"Feel them. Rough, like sand." Natsumi holds the pieces out to me. "Now you can see it really *was* a baby."

All too real. I had planned to say a few words, something about love; something also about loss.

But now, seeing tiny shreds of bone, my words seem meaningless, abstract.

As the three of us take the tiny pieces in our hands, I scatter them in the water and watch everything disappear.

The box empty, we hold each other, then sit staring at the lake and mountains. Natsumi takes off her wedge-heeled shoes and wades into the water. I watch as a light breeze catches her dress.

Red Beads

"ALL MOTHERS WORRY, it's only natural," my mother assured me, as we rode home from the hospital. This, I suppose, was in response to my multiple worries— cracked nipples, not having enough milk, the baby choking in its sleep. We were marvelling at our both being mothers when I looked at my newborn daughter and exclaimed, "How beautiful she is!"

I heard my mother's distinct, "No, she's not."

Surprised, I turned around. My mother had taken a bright red ribbon from her pocket, and was wrapping it around Rose's *tiny* wrist.

"Your Grandma Eva," she said, "used to make me wear a string of red beads. She always said the evil eye was attracted to red, that the beads were a decoy. It would go after the beads and leave me alone."

"And when I was little, did I wear something red too?" I asked.

"Oh yes. And whenever anyone mentioned what a beautiful child you were," said my mother, "or how smart, I quickly put you behind me and said you weren't, in case the evil eye might hear and try to destroy you."

THE SUMMER I TURNED NINE I found out my Grandma Eva had cancer, and that the cancer had spread.

I remember being in my mother's bedroom before the funeral. As she put on a black dress she said for the first time in her life she felt truly alone.

I touched her on the shoulder. "You have me," I said. "You have Daddy and Grandpa."

"No darling, that's not what I mean. I took her for granted."

She was there in the hospital when my grandmother died.

"If only," my mother said, "I could have talked to her. I always wanted her to hug me. I never realized I should have put my arms around *her*."

I tried to picture my grandmother—she'd never laughed or smiled—but saw instead a toy she had given me. A red and white plastic chicken. You pressed down on the chicken and out came an egg.

THAT SUMMER MY GRANDFATHER MOVED from their tiny apartment in the city and came to live with us.

We were to host a party. In the morning I'd helped my mother prepare platters of pigs-in-the-blanket and dips from Lipton's onion soup mix and sour cream. Later, when guests began arriving, I found my grandfather in his chair under a tall oak at the edge of the yard.

"A good day to you, young miss."

He greeted me as usual, tipping an imaginary hat.

"Aren't you coming to the party?" I asked.

"It's all right," he said, "I'm quite happy here. You just run along."

"But grandpa," I said, "I'd rather be with you."

He bent over in his chair, picked up a smooth grey stone. Held it out in his hand.

"Julie, do you know what will melt even a heart of stone?" he asked.

I smiled: my grandfather believed in miracles. "Kooky" was what my father called him. That morning I'd woken up to their voices in the kitchen. Going downstairs, I heard my grandfather begin one of his stories. "Your grandpa lives in another world," my father said, turning to me with a sigh.

"I mean 'stone' literally," my grandfather said.

He tilted his head slightly and I saw the pleasure on his face. I stared out over the yard silently. We lived in a blue and white house in the suburbs. Next door was a house exactly like ours but painted yellow, with the same neat lawn. A child had died in that house. I don't know when I first learned this. I can never picture our

25

house, though, without seeing the yellow one too. It is as clear in my mind as the tall oak under which my grandfather sat. The stone in his hand. The way he began telling me this story.

HE SAID, "A little girl was lost in the desert."

These, I remember, his exact words.

The girl—she was also nine—was trying to be brave, not crying, though she had been lost for some time.

Eventually, the girl comes across a statue of a woman in a grove of trees. Weary, she goes to it, lays down to rest. Soon a great emotion comes over her. "Mother! Where's my *mother?*" the girl cries. Just then one of her tears falls like a pearl on the feet of the statue. The stone woman comes to life, reaches down and holds the girl in her arms.

"So, Julie," my grandfather said. "What do you think of that?"

I said I found the story hard to believe. How, I said, could a tear make a statue come alive?

"It was magic. Or, maybe, not really." He tapped the stone in his hand. "There's nothing, nothing in the world," he said, "like a mother's love for her child."

"Was she the girl's mother then, the statue?" I wanted to know.

My grandfather smiled.

I said I hoped I'd never get lost in a desert without water. I didn't want to die. "Lucky, *she* didn't."

"Lucky, yes." He nodded. "Like you."

THERE ARE THINGS you don't remember. Bits and pieces you can't connect. A party. Red beads. A girl in a desert.

"I was an unmothered child," my mother has told me. "And so was my mother before me."

Was this the reason, then, for my grandfather's story?

Tears to remember.

Tears to break open a stone.

One cannot go back to sleep when one is weeping.

IN THE NIGHT thoughts come to you. You have arrived at motherhood late. You have only one child, a daughter. She still wakes up every few hours and you comfort her, nurse her back to sleep. Sometimes, looking over at your husband's face, you think you see her: she has his eyes, his light brown hair. Often, long after you've put her back in her crib, you feel you're still holding her in your arms.

Neapolitan

MY FATHER DRIVES FAST. He calls it the desire for con-
quest. He likes to pit his skills and the machine against
the elements. Stones on the road. A car coming from
one side. Wet leaves on a rainy night. "If it normally
takes an hour to get somewhere and you do it in half
the time," he once told me, "you're annihilating both
time and space."

This was in October 1962, when everyone worried
that the Americans would start a nuclear war in response
to Soviet missiles in Cuba, but all I could think about
was my parents' likely divorce. My father and I were in

his ham radio shack, my chair facing a picture of two apes writing the equation E=mc². Underneath the apes was the caption *Engineers ARE People*. As my father's tele-type machine clattered away with news signalling we were on the brink of war, I thought of those apes. They looked like mad scientists, scribbling furiously while a group of people stood by laughing, hands cupped over their mouths.

The apes had been there for as long as I could remember. My mother had a theory about the picture—she has a theory about everything. "The apes," she told me, "are actually intelligent extra-terrestrial life forms in disguise." Once, going past the door, she and I saw that my father had pasted an ice cream cone in the hand of one of the apes. "Theory has it," she said, "that if you crave dairy products, you were deprived of your mother's love." My father laughed.

My mother had something to say about everything, except my father's driving, that is. On long holiday trips we were captives in his Oldsmobile, racing down icy roads. Her face taut, one foot pressing an imaginary brake, she would turn to me in the back and whisper, "Isabel? Tell Daddy to slow down, okay? If I tell him he won't. You do it. Nicely."

When I tried he'd glance away from the road. "Your mother told you to say that, didn't she? Well, you can tell her I've got it under control."

I'd look at my mother, her eyes closed. Looking down, I'd see his small black polished shoe slowly press down on the gas.

ON THE PHONE NOW, twenty years later, my father and I make plans for his visit the last week of December. It's been ages since we've seen each other. When my parents finally divorced three months ago, he moved nearer to me—all the way from New York to Vancouver. And he has phoned just about every week.

Last week he agreed to take the plane, but today he says he'd rather drive. Because of the weather, only ten per cent of the planes are going out, he says. Vancouver Airport is at a virtual standstill. He points out it'll be much cheaper. Besides, he says, his health is improving. The last time he went in for tests they found only a small blockage in his carotid artery. "I could really see it, Isabel," he tells me. "I could see the blob right there on the screen. The equipment, you know, is quite remarkable."

When I mention the icy roads, the high mountain passes and the long drive, he scoffs at my "phobias" and tells me I'm as nervous as my mother. "You take the plane to Hong Kong or India, Isabel, not somewhere five hundred miles away." When I was a child he *did* go to these places. It seemed he was always away on business. I knew him from his post cards. *Having a good time. Going to Tokyo now. Love from your Dad.*

Then my father says he's placing a personal ad in the Vancouver papers.

"A personal ad?" I think of my mother's romantic account of their courtship. His tiny garret apartment cluttered with radio tubes. Their years of illicit pre-marital sex. How, though she had no interest in ham radio, she surprised him on their wedding day by producing her amateur radio license. He, for their first anniversary, gave her jade earrings in the shape of the number 88, "love and kisses" in amateur radio jargon.

He asks me now, "Would you mind, Isabel, if I consult with you over the phone?"

Mind? What am I going to say if my mother finds out about this? I can see her bitter smile. *How like him, so practical* I can hear her say. Will she blame me for collaborating? "Consult with you? Dad," I tease, "I'm not sure you can pay my fee."

He begins. "*Retired Gent, non-smoker, social drinker, loves classical music, computers, travel, seeks lady of similar interests for long-term close personal relationship . . . .* So," he asks me, "does that sound like your Dad?"

I laugh. "Why not include 'loves ice cream'?"

"Isabel. Be serious."

"Well, you certainly don't drink."

"Oh, I have the occasional beer now and then."

"Once a year?"

"The city is full of alcoholics. If I don't put in something about drinking, the ladies will think I'm a prude. Besides, if you have a beer sometimes, non-drinker isn't technically correct."

"Always the scientist," I laugh. When I went away to boarding school at fifteen, he sent me an anatomy and physiology text, along with a letter asking if I had any questions about sex. I wrote back *No*, though I was curious about the sample IUD, a Lippes Loop, that he'd slipped into the book. Even now I don't know where he got it.

"So now it's my turn," he says, and his voice softens, the way it always does when he approaches the subject of career or men. "How's the teaching going? Met any interesting guys?"

"No, no interesting guys," I reply in an off-hand way, "but the teaching's going well." There's a pause. I tell him then about the Christmas peace vigil I've been helping to organize. I'd like to ask if he'll go with me, but it is a delicate subject. I don't want it to become an issue if he says no. When I ask what he thinks of the speech I sent him—the one I plan to give at the vigil—he doesn't say anything.

Then, "Well dear, as I'm sure you know, I don't agree. But I don't disagree either."

What can I say? I'm beginning to think there is nothing that I *can* say when I hear my father's voice.

"Are you all right? You know I don't agree with you, a hundred per cent. I didn't like it when you moved to Canada with your draft-dodging boyfriend in the 60s and I don't like it now. But, I know you care deeply about the things you do."

I see him then, the way he used to look coming home, clothes rumpled, exhausted but exhilarated after working all night in his lab. And then it comes to me, what he always would say. "Isabel, it's important for the scientist to push *beyond* the frontiers of human understanding."

When I remind him now, he laughs. "Well, I certainly hope to make some contribution to society before I die."

"So do I, Dad," I say. "That's how I feel about what I'm doing too." I think of the small, dwindling peace group I attend, my commitment—and feel a sense of emptiness, regret.

"Can we talk, Dad? I mean, when you come to visit?"

"Of course, Isabel, we can always talk."

"And Dad—you will take the plane, won't you?"

"Okay, Isabel, okay," he concedes. "Only, promise you won't feed me any of your banana cream pie. My doctor has told me to lose fifty pounds."

MY MOTHER BELIEVES my father has come to terms with death. "Look at the way he drives," she says. "Is that the way a man who's afraid of dying drives?" My mother is a psychologist with an interest in Buddhist philosophy. She feels strongly that coming to terms with one's death is the single most important thing one can do. The last time I visited her she told me that peace activists—by which she means me—would never be successful until they came to terms with death. Personal death, that is.

We were in her new apartment, a month after the divorce. I had brought her several books—on despair, on empowerment, on genocidal mentality—which I'd been reading to make sense of it all and hoped to talk to her about. I meant to convince her personal and collective death were *not* the same thing. Look at my father.

I protested, "He can drive as fast as he wants, but what about us? We are all being taken on a ride we don't want to go on."

"So what? So what if your father believes nuclear weapons are necessary? People do."

"No," I said, "that's not the point and you know it. All those years you never once stood up to his driving, you had me do it for you. Even now, you won't commit your-

34

self or tell me you believe in what I'm doing. You'd rather give me some hogwash theory about inevitable failure."

"I'm not saying you'll fail, darling. Only that you need to go deeper into yourself. We all do. Even people trying to save the world."

My mother wants me to talk to him, tell him how I feel, make peace with him. "Isabel, he's your father," she says.

As I'm leaving, I see her sitting beside him in the Oldsmobile, her eyes closed as he races along, his small black shoe pressed down on the gas.

WHEN MY FATHER PHONES AGAIN, he has received eighty-seven replies to the ad and is interviewing three women a day—at breakfast, lunch and dinner—hoping to finish before he comes to visit. "Let me tell you, I'm not used to this," he says. "And I'm afraid my partners in crime are not helping me to lose any weight either."

I find it hard not to laugh. "It's because you kept 'social drinker'. The women think you're a lush."

"Isabel, be serious."

"Well, can't you take them out for a drive? How about a museum or concert? Or just a walk?"

I'm impatient with him, thinking, *He's never going to lose that weight, why try to change him?* when he says quite unexpectedly, "Well dear, what would you think if one of the ladies also wanted to come along?"

"Come here?" I ask.

"I always ask if they like driving," he says.

"Dad, we already agreed you wouldn't."

"What—invite someone?"

"No, drive. What about your heart condition? What about . . . ."

"I only said *if*. If I found a woman I liked. If she'd share the driving. You could meet her then, see what she's like. I'm meeting a lot of interesting ladies. Today I saw a marriage counsellor for breakfast, a cook for lunch, and for dinner, a cellist. The cellist is afraid of AIDS, hasn't had sex for five years."

"She told you that the first time you met?"

"Of course, Isabel. When I asked how she did without it, she said she masturbated."

"Honestly, Dad."

"Should I bring her?" he asks. "During the war she was one of Hitler's personal secretaries. But now she's a peacenik, like you. Think about it. She likes driving," he says.

HE PHONES NEXT FROM THE AIRPORT. His plane has been cancelled due to weather conditions; the next flight won't be in until tomorrow. He could *be* there tomorrow if he left right away, he says, in his car. But he can't—doctor's orders.

"What do you mean?"

"Look dear, it's nothing, really, nothing. When you're my age you come to expect things like this."

"Expect things like what? Dad, what on earth are you talking about?"

"I'm sorry, honey. I didn't want to worry you about it when I phoned. It happened several weeks ago, around your birthday. Just a minor heart attack, a little one," he says.

"Just a *little* one?"

"Actually, Isabel, I don't really think we need to talk about it now. But there is something I want to ask you. The woman I thought of bringing, the marriage counsellor—did I tell you she's thirty-nine?—can't come this weekend. There's another I quite like, but she isn't sure how you'd feel about our sleeping in the same room."

"The cellist?" I ask. "Hitler's secretary?"

"Former secretary. Should I bring her?"

"By all means, if you take the plane. You have to take the plane now, Dad, anyway. No matter what."

"Okay, boss."

"Dad, you know I'm really looking forward to seeing you. And I've got lots of food you can eat—shrimp, aspic—all kinds of things that don't have any calories at all."

"Only water, dear, has no calories," he says.

I laugh, then feel queasy. "Are you sure you're okay, Dad?"

"Look, I'm fine, but I'm in the airport and people are waiting. I'll see you soon. Tomorrow."

THE STEPS OF MY APARTMENT are slick with ice. My father descends them heavily, unevenly.

My father. Huge in his new jeans. I have never seen him in jeans. Tailored pants, suit jackets, starched white long-sleeved shirts, yes—but jeans? Never.

He talks about the women he has met. The restaurants he sampled with them. How his doctor has warned that he must go on a special diet. "But you know me, Isabel," he laughs.

I stop, facing him. "Would you like to sit down somewhere," I say, "to give your feet a rest?"

We walk another half block. A Christmas wreath exclaiming PEACE ON EARTH hangs on the restaurant door. Inside, red booths line the walls, and bunches of plastic holly dangle from the ceiling. I look at a menu. My father leaves his closed. I can tell he already knows what he wants.

"Ice cream for me," he tells the waitress. "Hot chocolate for you, Isabel?"

I think of the tossed green salad piled high with shrimp in my refrigerator. The tomato juice aspic made only this morning. The low sodium crackers bought especially for his visit. I should have known.

"Dad," I demand, "didn't the doctor tell you to lose fifty pounds?"

He nods contritely. "Why don't you get the ice cream, and *I'll* have the hot chocolate?"

When I was a child he'd order me one dessert after another—strawberry cheesecake, ice cream sundaes, pecan pie, whatever was available. When I said, "But Dad, you know I can't possibly eat all this!" he'd grin. "Don't worry, you've got *me*, honey. I'll help you out."

Now my father smiles at the waitress. "Tell me, miss, what would you recommend?"

"Me?" She throws her head back with a nervous laugh. "Why don't I bring a hot chocolate and ice cream and let you two decide?"

"That would be just fine," my father says as I look away, shaking my head.

"Very well, now that that's settled," says the waitress, amused, "which flavour? We've got vanilla, chocolate, or strawberry."

I look down. "Well then, a scoop of each, please," he says.

We sit quietly for awhile.

"Remember the times I used to sneak ice cream," he asks, "rescuing it from under the roasts and chicken in the deep freeze as soon as your Mom went to bed? I'm sure we devoured half a carton in each sitting."

His expression turns sober. He reaches down and rubs his legs for circulation, then loosens the laces of his black shoes.

"You know, Isabel, I can't walk the way I used to," he says. He looks at me with affection. "But, don't worry. I'll live a long time yet. Our family has a history of living well into our eighties. But even if I don't, I've had a good life, I've done what I've wanted."

"Yes Dad, I know."

I hesitate. On a piece of paper in my pocket I've listed several questions. How serious was the heart attack? Should I phone his doctor? What kind of diet should he be on? But these aren't my real questions. The real questions I can't find words for.

"Dad, you know you're killing yourself with all this ice cream," I say.

He laughs. "I'm a big boy. I can handle it."

There's a pause.

"Actually, dear, you'd be better off to worry about your own situation."

"Me?" I'm afraid now, like a child, as he presses his lips together, stern.

"It's not that I don't agree with what you're doing. We all want peace, don't get me wrong. But you can't spend your whole life giving speeches and going to marches, Isabel."

Silence.

"A woman your age should be thinking of marriage, having children. You shouldn't be so obsessed with the world's problems. You should be getting on with your life. I know these things are important to you, honey, but what I see is that you're not happy. And I want you to be happy. Why do you feel such despair?"

I shrug.

I hear myself talking. About treaties not ratified. The global arms trade. Computer accidents. He's not listening.

"Look honey, look at it this way," he says. "There are plenty of other things you could worry about too. How about plane accidents? People die every day just crossing the street. What if someone broke into your apartment? I notice you don't lock your door."

"No one needs to lock their doors here, Dad."

"Well," he says, "there's always a first time."

I feel frustrated. No, crushed. Trying to match his impeccable logic. Trying to beat him at his own game. I look down at the table, fumble with the napkin. I dab my eyes quickly.

"I'm sorry, dear. I didn't mean to upset you. You're really scared, aren't you, honey?"

I nod.

"Isabel, you really should try to think more positively." He squeezes one of my hands. "It's not going to happen."

"How can you be so sure?"

"Because," he says. "Rational people don't do those things."

"They might," I say.

"Yes, that's possible. But not probable."

I see my father's foot heavy on the gas pedal. I am silent. The waitress approaches with the hot chocolate and a large bowl with three scoops of ice cream. "Will there be anything else?" she asks.

"No thank you," he tells her. "You know, I really shouldn't be eating this. But Neapolitan—how lovely!"

As he dips into the bowl I watch his face fill with pleasure. I want to believe it's not too late. I want to tell him I love him. Pushing the bowl in front of me, he smiles.

"Go ahead," he says. "Go ahead."

Fire

His name is lenny and he wants to write a book. He wants to keep seeing you. "You're not a writer, you're a landscaper," you've told him, but since you don't use the same kinds of words Lenny uses, he thinks that you're smart. The first time he visits he takes a small notebook, memo size, the kind you use for shopping lists, from his rear pocket. He places, on your kitchen table, a mickey of rum.

"It's not going to be a book like some shrink would write. That's not my experience," Lenny says. "I don't know about shrinks. I only know things from deep inside."

43

You nod, reassure him. "Anyone can write their story. Everyone has something to offer."

"Yes," Lenny says, "I suppose."

Like you, he has a daughter; only his is fully grown. He married at seventeen, just out of high school. "I was young, young and stupid," Lenny says. "The marriage broke up and I went to Nam."

"But why?" you ask. "You're Canadian—you didn't have to."

Lenny puts some rum in his coffee and gives it a stir, says he went for the thrill.

No, "thrill" isn't the word he uses. What the exact word is you can't remember, though later you'll try, try to remember everything about this moment, when you first knew you liked him. Maybe because of his eyes—deep blue—that suggested vulnerability. Or was it an openness, a candour you found unusual?

"I like risky things. Fast cars. Sky diving." Lenny takes a sip of his coffee. "Sky diving is the best aphrodisiac. No, better."

He laughs. He looks at you in the way other men have. Young men. Older men. You've been on your own since your daughter was three. You have come to recognize it.

"So, ever tried bungee jumping?" you ask.

"No, not yet." Lenny smiles. "But once I did put out the lights in this town. Hang-gliding. I flew into the power lines and got caught in the wires."

He bends over and rolls up his jeans to show you the scars on the back of his legs where the wire cut into his flesh.

44

He takes your hand, places it on the swollen ridge of skin where the flesh scarred over.

"My God," you wince. "That must have hurt!"

"Oh no, I was out of it when they found me. I mean, blanked out completely. It was quite amazing. Really," he says.

AT SCHOOL, YOU GIVE your daughter Jessica a big hug and kiss; she hands you a half-sheet of bright yellow paper with the word "Notice." She tells you police visited her school.

"There was a big white van. Jill and Melody were grabbed," Jessica says.

"I saw the stranger. I saw him, Mummy. He was big and smoked cigarettes," she says. "Now we can't go outside at lunch."

You're not sure what to believe. She's six and has a vivid imagination. Jessica's afraid of men she doesn't know. Big men. Men with beards. Men who wear loose, dirty clothing. She's afraid of cigarettes too: people die from smoking. But Jessica's also afraid of witches, like the one with the green face in the *Wizard of Oz*. Witches pinch her in the night, she says. They sometimes tickle her under the arms.

You've tried educating her about safety. You review strategies regularly: "What would you do if a stranger offered you candy? What if he didn't offer you candy, but said Mummy asked him to give you a ride home? What if it wasn't a stranger who offered you a ride but one of Mummy's friends?"

Generally, you're pleased with Jessica's answers: "I don't like candy. I'd never go with a stranger—especially if he smokes! I'd say, 'What's our password?'"

Now, Jessica points excitedly to the notice. "Read what it says. Read it, Mum!"

Parents, you read to her. *There was an incident today at school. No one was hurt, and all in attendance have been accounted for. Police have been notified and advise you to drive your children both to and from school.*

You're glad the notice is so discreet and doesn't use a word like "rape" or "molest," words that come immediately to mind. You don't want to have to explain. Still, something about the notice leaves you dissatisfied.

"So, what did the police say, darling?" Feigning calmness, you smooth back your daughter's fine, light brown hair.

"They told us to scream as loud as we can and kick and run away fast. Wanta see how fast I run, Mum?" she beams.

❧

AN INCIDENT. AT LUNCH. This is what the principal tells you—you and some hundred-odd parents—in the gymnasium the following day. A white van was parked on the upper side of the schoolyard where two girls were playing. The driver offered the girls a "loonie" and some candy if they got in the van. The girls refused. The man came out of the van and tried to grab them. No one was hurt. The girls got away.

"So, was it *the* pedophile?" someone asks.

There's a moment of silence. Several weeks ago a convicted pedophile, released from prison, settled in

46

town. The pedophile—no one refers to him by name—is a local boy. He has been charged with indecent exposure, sexual acts—eleven offenses involving children under the age of eight. What kinds of offenses you've never asked.

When the pedophile, labelled by prison authorities as "dangerous, likely to re-offend," returned to live with his parents, there was a town meeting. The Mayor, city council and RCMP officers were all there. They told you they would be watching the man closely. The pedophile was prohibited from being near playgrounds, libraries, recreation centres and swimming pools—anywhere young children gathered. There was a court restraining order, they said.

Still, few felt convinced of their children's safety. When someone, a mother of three, shouted, "We want him out of town and now wouldn't be too soon!" the entire audience began clapping.

The RCMP officers were not pleased, they feared vigilante behaviour. No one wanted *that,* did they?

"We're not that kind of town. We never have been that kind of town," one of the officers said.

Now this officer stands beside the school principal, his hands, as though a shield, clenched tightly across his chest.

"Look, I understand how you people feel. But believe me, we're watching the man closely. And he wasn't anywhere near the school . . . ."

Then who was?

Yours is a quiet town. A clean, safe town at the end of the highway. You moved here with your daughter a year ago. In the city you were afraid to go out at night.

You were also afraid to stay home: what if someone came in through your window again?

The night was hot, a sweltering July night in the city. You slept naked under a sheet. Jessica, across the hall, wore your T-shirt with a big happy face on it.

That night, when you ran into her room naked, you couldn't find her at first. Jessica wasn't in her bed. She wasn't in the sheets coiled up in a mass on the floor. Then you opened the closet door and saw her crouching.

You were afraid; now you're angry. You thought it would be safer here.

A WHITE VAN? Lots of people have white vans; you now see them everywhere. The milkman. The baker. The carpet cleaner. The repairman for cable TV. White, you've just learned, is the safest colour for a vehicle. Lenny has a car that's white too. Sometimes he picks you up at work. Sometimes, when it's too hot to landscape anymore, Lenny comes for you early. One day his white Chevy is there at noon. The two of you go for lunch in the park.

Lenny talks about the book he's writing. About having found simple truths to live by. He talks about God. About Vietnam. He dreams about the war constantly. You've heard him shouting in his sleep. He wakes up in a cold sweat. But later he'll tell you in Vietnam he was most alive.

The war. Ordinarily, talking about it doesn't bother you. You've never known someone who's been in a war. In the past you've been full of questions. Now, though, you don't want to hear about it.

People are talking about incidents at other schools. A string of attempted abductions. Kids are scared; everyone's scared. The parents have organized a committee to take matters into their own hands. Some, you tell Lenny, are taking turns supervising at lunch. There's an after school buddy program in effect as well—senior high students matched with those in elementary school. Jessica's teacher has arranged for a self-defense class for girls and their mothers.

"Hey, calm down. Calm down. You've got me, remember?" Lenny puts an arm around you.

"You? What could you do?" You laugh.

"This self-defense stuff, I don't know. What if you fought back and it only made the person angrier? Couldn't a little bit of knowledge be dangerous? Couldn't you just . . . ."

"Act helpless? Play victim?" This is, of course, nothing new.

Lenny shrugs. "Well, *my* daughter never had any self-defense classes, and she grew up fine."

"Sure, but that's not the point. The point is—"

"She's managed okay. And she didn't need to learn any passwords," Lenny says.

"Not then, maybe," you say, "but times have changed."

Lenny looks down at his lap, then back at you. "I once killed a child, you know."

"A child?" You stare at him, speechless.

"A boy of ten. He was running behind me. A buddy of mine once got hit with a grenade like that. It was a child who threw it—completely obliterated everything below the waist. So I aimed at this kid and shot him."

"A child?" you say again. Lenny? He adores children. Hasn't he said he cares about Jessica as though she were his own flesh and blood?

"But I only had one nightmare about it. Guess I'm lucky," he says. "Only one."

❧

THE PEDOPHILE HAS BEEN SEEN hanging around the curling rink on "ladies night." You've heard he walks past your house every time he goes downtown. This you don't doubt: his parents live in a quiet tree-lined neighbourhood two blocks away.

But the police won't verify anything.

The first time you phoned about the curling rink, the officer said he wasn't concerned as long as there weren't any children involved. You play at the rink, you told him, Tuesday and Thursday nights. "I wasn't sure which was safer, to bring my daughter with me," you said, "or leave her with a babysitter at home."

This led to a second phone call. This time the officer was downright rude.

"I'm sorry lady, but the man's served his sentence. He's entitled to the same right to privacy as you or I."

"Even if he is the man at my daughter's school?"

"Well, we can't arrest him, can we," says the officer, "unless we catch him in the act."

Now you hear that the man at Jessica's school was wearing a blue baseball cap.

People tell you, "The two girls, Melody and Jill, gave a description."

And you want to ask: *what shade of blue? Was it light or*

dark? But what difference would that make? Lots of men have baseball caps that are blue; it's a common enough colour. Lenny has one with the letter "L" on it.

He was wearing that blue cap, come to think of it, the day you talked about the self-defense class. He wasn't so much against your taking it, no, but Jessica . . . ?

"Why destroy her childhood innocence?" he said. "Teach her to see men as the enemy."

You remember how he removed his blue cap then. Put a hand through his hair and sadly shook his head.

YOUR FIRST CLASS. A board is propped up on two blocks. Beneath it lies a soft pillow. "Aim for below the board, for the pillow," your instructor says.

Jessica's teacher, the first to split the board in two, has no trouble. The second to take her turn is a girl of twelve. Thwack. Her hand looks like a knife.

"Who's next?"

Your instructor puts her hands over yours. "Make a fist. Here, tighten it all the way up your arm," she shows you. "Now breathe. Breathe from your belly. Hit here, and remember: aim for below."

You hit—not once, but twice. Several times. The board stays intact. Your arm is in terrible pain. "Wait until next week," says your instructor. "Don't expect too much your first time."

You look around the circle at mothers and daughters facing you, at the twelve-year-old who has just taken her turn. Twelve, one-third your age. When you were twelve, your younger brother took Judo.

"I don't know. What if I just end up wasting everyone's time?" you shrug with a laugh.

Then Jessica's teacher says, "Think of Jessica. Think of someone grabbing your daughter."

You see Jessica's soft oval face. Remember how, when she was born, it was her eyes, deep pools, which drew you in while you nursed her. At night, you saw those eyes in your dreams. Bringing your fist down, you see them now.

Later you show Jessica the board split neatly into two.

"Oh Mum," she says, looking at you with those eyes, shiny amber. "Did you really do that?"

NOW IT'S AS IF you're all antennae. You walk down the street looking every man in the eye. You stare at men's bodies, thinking, *If I had to protect myself, where would I hit?* Even Lenny's body, which has given you pleasure, you look at in a new way, a way you never imagined possible.

A blow to the temples takes three pounds to kill.

Fifteen pounds can crush a knee.

Splitting the board, you used about thirty pounds—but the average woman is capable of eighty. *Eighty* pounds when the adrenalin starts pumping!

You tell Lenny how excited you feel. You've never experienced such power.

You say: "It's indescribable, the way every cell's working . . . ."

Lenny wants to hear more, he wants to hear everything, but he can't help being a tease.

"Oh yeah, you're gonna beat me up! I'd better be careful now." He laughs, throwing you down on the bed.

You're laughing too. "Hold me here. Put your arms around me like this." Lenny does. With a quick twist of the wrist you surprise him, releasing his hold.

Lenny loves it. He loves it.

But it doesn't turn you on. "I don't like this, Lenny, please." His hands are rough. Lifting your blouse, he starts kissing your breasts.

EIGHTY-FIVE PER CENT of sexual assaults on women are by a male known to her.

One woman is raped every seventeen minutes in Canada.

Age and appearance do not matter. Anyone can be assaulted—from small babies to women over ninety.

This last fact, for some reason, you find surprising. The day Lenny raped you, you were wearing something provocative—a halter top, tight black jeans.

"The problem between men and women," you tell him, "is one of power."

"What power?" says Lenny. "My father was an alcoholic, he abused us terribly. If we even asked to go to the bathroom we'd get a lickin'."

"You see?" you say. "You see what I mean? It's a culture of male violence."

Lenny calls what happened a "misunderstanding."

HE FOLLOWS YOU TO WORK, to Jessica's school. He walks a half block behind you, or drives slowly in his car.

When you come home there are flowers on your front steps. The phone rings as you open the door.

"I love you, can't you see how much I love you?" Lenny whispers in your ear.

"Stop bothering me. Leave me alone," you reply.

But Lenny won't. He's a fighter. A fighter from way back, he tells you. "You're not going to get rid of me that easily. I care about you. You're the first person I've cared about for a long time," Lenny says.

A DOZEN ROSES—three white, three pink, three yellow, three red.

Carnations—pink and white variegated. Baby's breath.

Lenny stands across the street from your house, watching as you open the box.

He stands there, waving, watching.

You walk to the side of the house, open the lid to the garbage can, and throw the flowers in.

Months pass. The flowers keep coming. You no longer see Lenny watching from across the street, but you sense he's still there.

Years from now the flowers will arrive only on the anniversary of your first night together. Your name will appear on the dedication page of Lenny's book.

In the book, the man continues to send the woman he loves flowers. When she walks to school to pick up her daughter, he follows her in his car. This leads to a scene in which the woman pounds angrily on the car window. The man asks her to get inside the car—maybe they can talk. Suddenly he's pleading with her to take him back and she's in the seat beside him thinking maybe he's crazy. "Let me out of here! Let me out!" she screams, but the man won't, and he locks all the doors. The woman starts a fire, takes a lighter to a newspaper lying on the seat.

Never yell "help" because people will run. Yell "fire" if you want help.

Fire was all you could remember. That's how you managed finally to get free, unlock the door.

The Age of Analysis

Inappropriate Behaviour
To Be Young, To Be Beautiful
Rapture

Inappropriate Behaviour

SEVERAL MONTHS BEFORE she stopped working on the psych ward, Ellie dreamed she was in the Quiet Room. At first she thought it was the Operating Room because the light from the ceiling was so bright and the room so cold. Ellie felt sick, as if she'd been given an anaesthetic, though she couldn't think of what kind of operation she'd had. Then something changed and the wall turned into a window with bars. She saw the thick steel door open and Liz came in, and behind her, Joan, the head nurse. It wasn't clear just what they were going to do to her.

The next morning at work when she told them her dream, the two nurses laughed.

"That's ridiculous. Why would we ever put you in Room 11?" Liz lit a cigarette, blew smoke rings in the air.

Joan was quiet. "Honestly, Ellie," she said, shaking her head.

THERE ARE TIMES NOW, months after leaving the psych ward, that Ellie thinks of the dream. Just what were Liz and Joan about to do? Anything she tries to imagine seems absurd.

"This is a modern ward," the head nurse proudly told her a year ago at her job interview. They didn't use shock treatments and gave medication only when necessary. "What I'm looking for," Joan said, "is someone who cares about people."

THE QUIET ROOM was at the end of the hall. It had two doors. The outer door, number 11, displayed the word SECLUSION in white letters on a brown Formica plaque. When it was unlocked, you stepped into a small antechamber. Inside were a basin and seatless toilet. The second door was made of thick steel with a key lock, bolt and peephole. When Ellie stood in front of the steel door her first week on the ward, she heard a voice calling for help.

Joan said: "Liz, you carry the tray. Ellie, you empty the urinal bottle. I'll do the talking."

Liz's tray held a small plastic medicine cup and a hypodermic needle; Joan carried a blood pressure cuff. Neither looked like nurses. Liz, tall and blonde, wore a silk blouse, beige skirt and suede heels. Joan wore a modest navy pant suit and gold cross at her neck. Ellie, who'd hoped to develop rapport with the patients in her casual sweater and corduroy pants, had been mistaken by the janitor that morning for a new admission.

Looking through the peephole in the door, Joan said, "He's not on the mattress." She turned to Liz; their eyes met. Joan nodded and turned back to the steel door.

"Harold," she said firmly, "Would you lie down? Please lie down on your mattress."

Suddenly Liz jumped to one side, nearly tripping over Ellie's feet.

"Sorry, didn't mean to alarm you," Liz said. "I just thought I saw his hand reach through the food tray hole."

"The *what?*" Ellie's legs felt like rubber. Liz pointed to their feet. At the bottom of the steel door was a hole about six inches high, wide enough for a hospital food tray.

"Don't get too near that hole. If he's not on the mattress he might grab you," Liz said. "There've been people who could get half their body through it."

"Half a body?" Ellie stared at Liz, wondering if she was joking. "You mean an arm?" she said. "Or maybe a leg?"

"Shhhh." Joan looked through the peephole. "Could you two be quiet?" She put a finger to her lips, then motioned for Ellie to join her.

Ellie stood back from the food tray hole and squinted with her eye against the tiny peephole. The body on the mattress was distorted, as though seen in a convex circus mirror. She took a deep breath to calm herself, trying to remember what she knew about Harold—which was virtually nothing.

❧

ELLIE HAD GRADUATED from nursing school with a whopping student loan to pay off and felt fortunate to get the job. Initially, she'd had misgivings. She'd heard stories about what went on in psych wards. She tried to tell Joan at the interview that she had little experience in psychiatry, but the head nurse only shrugged. "You strike me as an honest, caring person. If my intuition's correct, patients will feel that way too."

Patients took to Ellie immediately. They confided in her over games of cards. They laid bare their life histories while crocheting afghans. Each day Ellie learned to bake something new—scones, sweet rolls, cream puffs. She started to macramé plant hangers. Soon she was knitting socks. The psych ward wasn't like other wards. Nurses didn't wear uniforms. They didn't change beds, give bedpans or do sterile dressings.

There were, however, endless forms to fill out. Every detail of patients' lives had to be noted—how they ate, slept, participated, met goals the nurses set. The charts followed a formula—problem, goal, plan, outcome—but most problems were as simple as loneliness.

Liz and Joan liked the paperwork. Both spent hours in the nurse's station while Ellie sat with the patients. And then one morning, as Joan was finishing a patient's chart, Ellie asked if they could talk.

"I'm really enjoying the ward. The only thing is . . ." Ellie hesitated. "Isn't there something more I should be doing?"

"Don't worry, you're doing fine," Joan told her. "Still, strange you should mention this. Just a minute ago Liz and I were talking. There's been some trouble with Harold in the Quiet Room. We weren't going to ask you, you're so new. But we could use your help."

"The guy in Room 11?"

"Not to worry." Joan smiled encouragingly. "Just take a look at his chart and you'll be fine."

Twenty-one-year-old patient admitted for having premonitions. Feels state of moods correspond to tensions in world politics, e.g. recent 'space war' in Middle East. Follows news on transistor radio incessantly, analyzing it.

This wasn't the whole story, Ellie thought. Harold hadn't attacked anybody. He hadn't jumped off a bridge. Why lock him up?

Liz thought it had to do with Harold's radio. When she took it away during his admission, saying she'd put it in the nurse's station for safe-keeping, Harold became frantic. He had told her the reason he kept it on low was so it wouldn't bother anyone. He actually screamed at her, "Is it a crime to keep a radio on low?"

Ellie asked why Liz hadn't simply returned the radio. Liz laughed. "You really think that radio was *on?* Come on, kiddo, he's listening to voices."

Spends time listening to radio which does not appear to be on. Apparently hallucinating.

Below Liz's words, the head nurse had written: *Denies hallucinating.*

"We ask everyone who comes in 'Do you hallucinate? Do you have delusions?' If the patient says no," Joan told Ellie, "just record *denies* on the chart."

"But if you write *denies*," she said, "doesn't it sound

63

like they're not telling the truth? What if Harold isn't hallucinating?"

"Everyone writes *denies*, Ellie." Joan's tone was blunt. "It's standard practice."

❧

THE QUIET ROOM was cold and smelled of urine. A few pink tissues which had been used to try to wipe it up lay shredded on the floor. Ellie went to open the window, but it was block glass behind bars.

Joan said, "We want to take your blood pressure. Then we'll give you something to calm down."

She wrapped the cuff around Harold's arm. Harold moved on the mattress.

"Hey, what's this you're giving me?"

He spoke slowly, as if in a daze. He was small-boned and slender, with dark eyes and dark hair pulled back in a ponytail.

"Your blood pressure is fine." Joan ripped the cuff off his arm. "Now we want you to take your medication." She signalled with her eyes for Liz to bring the cup of liquid.

"Hey, wait a minute," said Harold.

Joan offered the cup. "If you don't take this," she said, "we'll have to give you an injection."

"Forget it." Harold jerked his head away.

"I'll get a mop," Ellie said.

"A mop?" Joan looked perplexed.

"A mop. Yes, a mop," Ellie heard herself babble. The light from the ceiling made her head ache. The smell of urine made her dizzy. "When I see a mess like this—"

"Shouldn't you empty the bottle first?" Joan said.

"The bottle? Oh yes, the bottle." Ellie picked up the urinal bottle which had overflowed and took it to the toilet in the antechamber. She turned on the tap and slowly and repeatedly rinsed the bottle.

When she returned, Harold was on his stomach. Liz put the used syringe on her tray.

"SO, YOU THINK we should just let him out?" Dr. Cooper asked Ellie back in the nurse's station.

Dr. Cooper stared at her. He was in his fifties and wore a black shirt under a blue jacket. Earlier that week the psychiatrist had introduced himself. "Call me Barry," he said, lifting her hand as if to kiss it. Now Ellie wasn't sure whether she could tell him what was on her mind.

"About Harold. Would you say his behaviour was appropriate?" Dr. Cooper asked.

Ellie frowned. She shrugged. "Just what do you mean by appropriate?"

Dr. Cooper took a pink sheet of paper off a shelf labelled "Emergency Commitments." On the back of the paper he wrote *schizophrenia*, underlined once, and below it *behaviour*, underlined twice; then a list:

a) *inappropriate*
b) *manneristic*
c) *unpredictable*
d) *regressive*

He put the list in front of her on the table and said, "Well? Which category would you say he falls into?"

Ellie looked up at the ceiling and laughed. "Are you serious?"

Dr. Cooper said, "Come on, if you don't know, take a guess."

"Is he dangerous? Is that why he's in there?"

"Oh no, not dangerous, just a bit muddled," Dr. Cooper replied.

"But I don't understand," Ellie said. "You wrote *paranoid schizophrenia* on his chart."

"Well, we need an admitting diagnosis."

"But Seclusion?"

Dr. Cooper shrugged. "This is an open ward. He tried to run away once. We're afraid he might try again."

"But he's twenty-one, an adult, and if he hasn't committed any crime . . . ."

"Actually, Ellie, it's not that simple. He's so unpredictable we don't know what to do. We're babysitting."

"Babysitting?"

"I'm afraid that's all we can do under the circumstances," Dr. Cooper said. "When the police picked him up at a peace demonstration, Harold was soliciting donations for an organization that doesn't exist. The police confiscated the money. Harold put up a fuss. He'll tell you the organization exists, he only made a mistake in the wording. He also thinks the police took a thousand dollars from him, if you can believe that."

"But you can't just keep him in there . . . ." Ellie shook her head. Dr. Cooper was taking his time, being patient. But then: "Maybe you're right. Maybe we should let him out anyway," Dr. Cooper said. "They get the idea they're being punished when you keep them in there too long."

"CUT OUT AND PASTE things that have meaning to you. We'll talk about them later," Liz instructed the Awareness Group the following day while Ellie passed out sheets of white paper and magazines. But Ellie, working on her own collage, soon tired of Kraft cheese slices, Campbell's soup, dog food and cats. She started cutting out slogans. SHAPE UP! KEEP FIT! She glanced at Harold's blank paper.

"Here, try these." Ellie passed him two slogans: NO COMMITMENTS! NO KIDDING!

Harold smiled. "Thank you. I needed that."

"No problem. Any time," Ellie laughed.

She supposed Harold thought she was the one who'd gotten him out of the Quiet Room. She felt flattered. He was attractive; he had a wonderful smile. There was a mischievous gleam in his eyes when he talked, and he talked constantly; he had theories about everything.

"Say today is Monday," he said, "and the rule this morning is you've got to do everything with your left hand."

Harold shifted the scissors from his right hand to his left.

"This is a schizophrenic story, a left-handed story."

He told her his dog's name was Rebecca. She was four years old and had black hair. He and the dog thought about each other, but he knew she hated him because she yapped all the time.

"I didn't love her enough to train her, even though she's four years old," Harold said. "You see, Rebecca's half-wild because her father's name was Danny, and he was a wild dog. She's also a half-breed Venusian."

He looked at Ellie and smiled.

"You're beautiful," he said suddenly.

"What?"

"I mean it. The moment I saw you I knew you'd help me."

He took Ellie's hand. His was warm, and when she looked into his dark eyes Ellie felt a warm glow. She glanced across the room and wondered if Liz was watching. From a distance she heard a pen tapping the counter, Liz calling, "Could everyone please hold up your paper now and describe it? Everyone please stop."

Harold squeezed her hand, then let go of it. When he held up his paper, Ellie could tell Liz was not pleased.

Liz shook her head at him, but once they'd gone around the circle she seemed to have forgotten why.

"What shall we do tomorrow? How about a debate?" Liz asked. "Any ideas?"

❧

AFTERWARDS, IN THE NURSE'S STATION, Liz kept her distance from Ellie, pursing her lips. Ellie wondered if Liz was still upset because of the slogans. She asked if anything was the matter, but Liz wouldn't say.

"Look, be honest," Ellie told her.

"Okay," Liz said. "I was wondering what you were doing with Harold. I saw you talking in the Activity Room. Then holding hands."

"Don't you ever touch patients?" Ellie asked.

Liz laughed, then said, "If it's just chitchat, I don't see any problem."

"Well, that's all it is," Ellie told her.

"Okay. But chitchat can soon turn into problems. If you know what I mean."

"What kinds of problems?" Ellie asked.

Liz shook her head. "All kinds, kiddo. You'll see."

THAT WAS THE NIGHT of Ellie's dream. The next morning, after she told Liz and Joan about it, Joan assigned Ellie to give out medications. "To take your mind off things."

All morning Ellie felt something about to go wrong. Carrying her tray, she called "Pill-time!" the way she had seen Liz and Joan do. The patients assembled in the day room. To Ellie, their voices seemed happy, nearly euphoric:

"I'm only on twenty-five milligrams."

"Well, I'm on fifty."

"*She* only gets ten—can you imagine!"

And so on. Were they boasting, Ellie thought, or voicing some kind of complaint? She handed them their pills in a Lily cup.

"Harold?" she called. "Harold, where are you?"

No sign of him in the TV room or Activity Room. Nor in the consultation room or kitchen. Standing with her pill tray, Ellie looked out the large day room window.

"How clever of them, to make you look like a waitress."

The voice behind her was low, muffled and strange. Turning around, Ellie was startled to see him. "Oh there you are," she said brightly. "Only two pills for you this morning!"

Harold came closer. Ellie wasn't sure of the look in his

eyes. She watched him carefully. What was this, some kind of joke?

"Here, sir, are your jelly beans!" Ellie tried to laugh. She held the Lily cup out to him with a smile.

His eyes narrowed, his body stiffened. "I don't like the food you carry on your tray."

Food? Was he hallucinating? "Look, if you have any dietary complaints," she said, imitating the calm, reasonable nurse's voice she'd heard Liz use, "I'm sure the kitchen staff will listen. But these are pills."

"Can I have my cigarettes now? Can I have my razor?" he said quietly, the words monotone.

Why was he talking like this? Ellie felt her face flush; she was beginning to sweat.

She took a ball from the ping-pong table nearby. "The doctor's just prescribed this. I know it's hard to swallow, but do the best you can."

"You think you're cute, don't you?" he said in a whisper. "You really think you're different from the rest."

Ellie tried to talk to him, but he knocked the tray out of her hands.

"It's poison! Poison!" he screamed at her. "You'll make me sick!"

❧

TUESDAYS WERE BRIDGE. Wednesdays were sing-songs. Thursday was bowling, but only when the patients were good. Harold was back in Room 11.

"I told him he'd be allowed out of the room as soon as we gave him his clothes," said Dr. Cooper.

"Oh," laughed Liz, "and what did he say?"

"He said he didn't need his clothes. In fact, he was beginning to feel better already without them. He suggested I take off my clothes, that all the nurses take off their clothes. He said walking around in pajamas could make a world of difference to how you were feeling."

To Be Young, To Be Beautiful

SATURDAY. NATHAN IS BACK.

He liked being away. Eight weeks with a crew in the mountains. Mosquitoes, black flies, rain; the hot muggy work. He felt needed by the others. He could go into the mess tent after coming down the hill. He could listen to them play guitar and joke. He could watch.

SUNDAY HE SPENDS HOURS dyeing her underwear. Corals, blue-greens and purples. He wants to see it on her.

"Tell me to choose a pair of underwear," Nathan says. She doesn't answer, she's just getting out of the bathtub. "Ellie?"

"Okay," she says.

He goes into the bedroom, looks in the drawer at the bright array of colours and textures: elasticized nylons, opaque cottons, terry cloth. He brings her a pair of orange Dayglo bikinis and watches as she puts them on.

Nathan always chooses.

"DO YOU KNOW about the Dyaks of North Borneo?" Nathan asks.

No, Ellie doesn't know. It is a Monday morning, before work.

"Be quick. I've only got fifteen minutes," she says.

"Well, the Dyaks of North Borneo," says Nathan, "increased women's enjoyment of sex by scarring the head of men's penises to produce greater friction in intercourse."

"Oh my God. Really?" Ellie is shocked.

"Yes. Let me show you the book."

"No don't. How painful." She winces.

"Just think, Ellie, female-dominated cultures have always existed, hope for the future."

LATE TUESDAY AFTERNOON Nathan takes her hand, guides her up steep, rocky terrain to the site where he will build her friend a solar home.

"Have you built many of these before?" Ellie asks.

"I did once. But with men. You know, a straight nine to five job."

Ellie nods, careful to watch where she is going. Ahead lie sharp jagged boulders. She imagines molten rock at her feet, thick black lava.

"I think men don't relate to each other emotionally like women do. This job'll be different, working with a woman."

"It's different working with just any woman?"

Nathan stops on the rock above her. He cups his hand over his eyes and stares out at the purple-green mountains.

COUVADE. THERMONDONTINES. BLACK EGG. KAURI. Wednesday she reads aloud words she's never seen before. "What's this book about, Nathan?"

He smiles. "How destiny has been thwarted by the conquests of men," he says solemnly. "Here, give it to me."

Opening it to the title page, he inscribes:

For Ellie,

This book showed me what it means to be a whole person.
            Love, Nathan

NATHAN'S KNOWLEDGE DOES NOT STOP with the Dyaks of North Borneo. He also knows everything about cameras, flying airplanes, skiing (Nordic), cooking Chinese, the I Ching and tie-dyeing sheets.

Thursday, when Ellie calls in sick, they put the sheets in the dye bath and let them boil for several hours while they lie in bed. Later he rinses them while she makes omelettes, filled with spinach, mushrooms, zucchini, olives and mozzarella. While they are eating he shows her the small shell he keeps in his pocket.

It has a red, smooth opening.

"What is this?" she asks.

"A kauri shell. Some women carry it for good luck."

Ellie holds the shell in her hand. It is pale brown with white spots. Putting it against her ear, she hears the roar of the ocean.

"This is a faun kauri. There are other kinds as well, arabic or snake, but I prefer the faun kauri," Nathan says.

As he tucks the shell in its maroon suede pouch, she glimpses the light fur on his belly. She reaches out and touches its softness. As soft, she imagines, as a young faun.

"I DON'T WANT to talk about it."

"Oh really. Why?" Nathan asks. "You're not mad at me for something, are you?"

"No, course not. Why should I be?"

She sits down at the kitchen table.

"Well, you seem like you're angry," Nathan goes on.

"Well I'm not. I just don't enjoy all these questions."

"I can tell you're upset about something, Ellie. What's going on? Tell me. What happened at work?"

Nathan hates the work she does, but he's out of a permanent job and four thousand dollars in debt. Even so, he thinks she should never have started nursing on the psychiatric ward. He thinks her work is immoral. Shooting people up with Thorazine, behaviour modification, and the rest of it.

"I'm tired. Just tired," she says.

"Your voice is high-pitched. You're all hunched over. Here, stand up. Let me straighten your shoulders."

She sighs, burying her face in her hands, then stands dutifully as Nathan pulls back on her shoulders.

"There. Feel any better now?"

"A little." Appeasing him, she sits down.

"Your voice still sounds weak. What's going on with you?"

"Nothing. I already told you. Look, it's really nothing. I've only been there a few months. If I really hate it, I'll switch."

"Dammit Ellie, why don't you let go?"

She sighs. "What do you want me to do? Scream?"

"Sure, if that will help. You can't scream there, but you can here."

"I can't. I feel numb."

"You feel angry!" Nathan prompts.

"Oh Christ."

"Dammit Ellie, don't let them do this to you. Don't just sit there feeling weak and powerless. Admit it. You're outraged by what goes on there, by the way they treat women. You're angry!"

"Numb!" she says louder.

"Angry!" Nathan challenges.

"Numb!"

"You feel pissed off. Admit it!" he demands, towering over her, his eyes fixed, his body rigid with rage.

"Stop it! Leave me alone!" she screams, terrified.

Nathan takes a step back. "I'm only trying to help you," his wet, grey eyes plead.

THE PARTY SATURDAY NIGHT is at Peggy's. At one of Peggy's earlier parties a man put his arm around Nathan. Slender and slight, they looked a lot alike. Nathan can't understand why people think he's gay.

As Ellie and Peggy stand by the hors d'oeuvres, a gay couple approach, hand in hand.

"Good evenin' ladies. You all enjoyin' yourselves?" one of the men says in an affected Southern accent.

"Oh yes," says Peggy.

"Well that's fine, just fine," he says.

The two men mingle. One wears a blond wig and a long, red gown. The other wears a white gown fitting snugly over his falsies.

"Aren't they a riot?" says Peggy. "Will you take a look at those red pumps?"

Ellie nods. As she reaches for her third egg roll she feels a pair of hands on her waist. She turns around quickly.

"Jill!"

A woman in a thin jersey T-shirt smiles.

"Wanna dance?"

"Sure," Ellie says.

Jill takes her hand and leads her onto the dance floor. A few minutes later Jill reaches into her pocket for a small bottle she lifts to her nostrils. "Want some?" she says, inhaling.

"What is it?"

"Amyl nitrate. You tried it?"

"No."

"Well then, you're in for a surprise." Jill holds out the bottle. "Gives you multiple orgasms, right on the dance floor."

"Thanks, maybe later."

Jill laughs. "Suit yourself," she says, passing the bottle on.

NATHAN CAN'T STAND IT.

"I won't have this," Nathan shouts Sunday afternoon when Ellie returns to the apartment. "We agreed to destroy monogamy. We agreed to sexual equality. You can continue sleeping with as many men as you like. But *this* isn't part of our agreement."

"What about open relationships, loving other people so that our relationship grows?"

She looks at his icy expression, his rigid shoulders. She thinks about how inconspicuously this man has walked into her life. He'd said once, "There are so few conscious people in the world so it's not surprising, is it, that the conscious ones seek each other out?"

Now Ellie sees terror in Nathan's face as he measures his words carefully.

"If you think I'll stand by and watch you, you're

wrong. I won't. I refuse to stand by and watch you falling in love."

Nathan, such an unaccountably serious lover.

JILL AND ELLIE. Nathan has been lovers with both of them, so why, Ellie asks, is Nathan so upset?

"I don't trust her," he says. "She uses men. She doesn't really like them. Deep inside she's not bi, she's really a lesbian."

"So?" Ellie says. "So are a lot of women you've slept with. What difference does it make?"

"She'll turn you against me. She's no friend of mine."

"Does someone have to be your friend first in order for me to like them?"

Nathan takes a step backward. "I can see you don't understand. You don't have any idea what I'm saying."

"You want me to stop being Jill's lover because you're paranoid."

Nathan's cold grey eyes focus on her. "You realize what this means."

"Yes. You're going."

Nathan nods.

"So, are you going to see Christine?"

"Maybe."

"Not maybe. Definitely."

"Well, okay then, yes. At least Christine is a friend."

Ellie laughs. Christine has long chestnut hair and eyes that are hazel or sometimes green. She lives by herself in a cabin she built outside Dawson Creek and has good muscle tone from hauling water and handling axes.

Nathan once told Ellie that he found Christine very sexually exciting.

"I need space," says Nathan now. "I'm going."

"Well, what are you waiting for? Go then," Ellie says.

Nathan throws a few things into a beat-up blue knapsack and grabs the pillow he's had since he was three.

"Goodbye," he says, slamming the door behind him.

He'll be back soon enough.

Rapture

"Do you like my robe and sandals?" Ken asks. He pirouettes in front of Ellie, displaying a striped kaftan, rope belt and brown leather thongs.

"I'll be glad to get my clothes back before I'm crucified," he says. "Know what I mean about being *crucified,* Ellie?"

Ken winks at Dr. Cooper, who smiles as Ken hands Ellie a calling card. On one side is a pen-and-ink sketch of Jesus in a neatly trimmed beard; on the other, a quotation from the Bible, carefully handwritten: *The Day of the Lord will come like a thief. The heavens will disappear with a roar. The elements will be destroyed by Fire, and the earth and everything in it will be laid bare.* (2 Peter 3:10)

"You know," he says, "Today could be the Day of the Lord. Or it could have been yesterday, the day of my flight. I took a great risk in taking the plane. We could have all been killed. What if both pilots had been Christian? What if they had *raptured* at the same time?"

"Raptured?" Ellie asks.

"Been transported to heaven on the Day of Judgment. The Day of the Lord. And I would have been left on the plane to crash to my death." He comes close to Ellie and looks her straight in the eye. His kaftan drapes open to reveal a yellow hospital gown.

"But Ken," she says, "what do *you* have to worry about? Wouldn't you, being a good Christian, rapture too?"

UNLIKE THE OTHER PATIENTS, Ken doesn't get needles or pills. He's served coffee from the staff room, on a silver-plated tray which Dr. Cooper offers as they chat for hours in his office.

This has gone on for three days. When other patients say, "I want to see the doctor, how come I don't see the doctor?" Dr. Cooper sits down with them for a few minutes in the day room.

"You'll have to be careful with this one, Ellie," he cautions her, his voice low as the two of them leave Ken in the day room. "He's a brilliant criminal lawyer, and we don't want a malpractice suit on our hands. Of course, don't believe everything he says. He may try to manipulate you."

"What about the wife?" Ellie asks with concern. "Did he say why he beat her?"

"No," Dr. Cooper shrugs. "Amnesia, I'm afraid."

"Four broken ribs, contusions everywhere, and he can't remember?" she says. "Come on, doctor." Since she's been on the ward, Ellie's seen a few cases she thought Dr. Cooper misdiagnosed, but nothing this bad.

The doctor shakes his head. "Ellie, this is a sick man. The irritable hyperactivity, the elevated drive? The way he talks, shouts and swears constantly? He can't help himself, he's a classic manic-depressive, completely out of control."

"You really believe that?" Ellie asks. "I'm not convinced. I think he knows perfectly well what he's doing."

He starts sorting through papers on the desk, then looks up, waiting for her to go.

This is not the first time Dr. Cooper has taken her aside. Once he commented on her "unprofessional" green corduroy pants. Another time, about her peace button, teasing that cigarettes were more lethal than bombs.

"Of course," Dr. Cooper says now, "Ken could leave us and be released back into police custody. Instead, he's chosen to stay awhile and try to cope with his illness, gain some insight."

"Insight?" Ellie says. "You really think he'll gain insight, with a history like his?"

J. Kenneth Egleton, a prominent Calgary lawyer, assaulted his wife while vacationing on Vancouver Island. People in the hotel room next to them heard her cries and phoned the police. When they arrived, the wife was unconscious, the lawyer naked except for a kaftan and sandals. On seeing the police, he fell down on his knees, flagellating himself with a piece of rope and begging for God's forgiveness. The police, evaluating his mental fitness before pressing charges, brought him in for a forty-eight-hour psychiatric review.

◆➤

IN THE TV ROOM, Ellie feels a light tap on her arm. "I would like my razor now. Oh I promise, I won't hurt anyone. I'm no danger to myself or others," Ken says.

He winks with his left eye, twice, at Gladys. Gladys is an Organic Brain Disorder and doesn't understand. She came in a few days ago for tests. Sometimes Gladys has startling moments of clarity, but last week she left the gas on in her kitchen and nearly burned her house down.

"I'll have to ask the doctor first, Ken," Ellie says. "There are rules, you know."

"That *doctor* is trying to label me but he's way off base. Know what I mean?"

Ken winks again, this time at Harold, a twenty-one-year-old schizophrenic. Harold, whose moods correspond to tensions in world politics, is constantly analyzing the news. Right now he's following the war in the Persian Gulf on TV, as well as on a transistor radio held close to his ear. Harold has trouble with boundaries; he's not clear where the fighting is.

"You know, Harold," says Ken, "Armageddon is not to be feared by the righteous."

Harold turns up the volume on his radio.

"When the world teeters on the brink of calamity, when Israel's enemies seek to destroy her," Ken lifts his hands and says loudly, "God will intervene."

Gladys looks confused.

Ken raises his arms high, as if offering benediction. "The heavens will open. All true Christians will be snatched away from this world and rapture. Be transported to heaven."

"Oh," says Gladys, "I think I'd like to rapture too."

"All our dreams reduced to rubble," says Harold, shaking his head.

At this, Gladys starts waving her hands and stamping her feet. "Why can't I rapture?" she yells at Harold. "I can *so* rapture if I want to!"

Ken winks again, this time at Ellie.

"Hey Ken, what's a matter with your eye?" Gladys asks.

Ellie explains. "It's something he does when he's saying one thing to one person but there's someone there who understands what he's *really* saying. So he winks to show they understand each other. Got it?"

Gladys still looks confused. "Can you do it with your other eye too?"

Ken winks with his left eye at Harold, then at Gladys with his right.

❧

KEN WANTS TO SPEND MONEY. He wants to take the patients downtown and buy them gifts at Woolco, but no one will go. It's week two of the Gulf War, and everyone is watching the news.

"What do you need?" he calls into the TV room.

"Cigarettes," says Gladys.

"Cigarettes are bad. Eat an apple," Ken says.

He opens a yellow canvas bag slung over his shoulder and hands Gladys an apple. Gladys, a chain smoker, turns away.

"Apples. I'd much rather give you apples, my children."

Ken empties the canvas bag full of apples onto the floor. They roll under the furniture. No one pays any attention.

On the TV bombs explode. President Bush talks about surgical strikes, high tech weaponry, laser bombs, computer-guided SMART missiles attacking their targets.

"Look, the Battle of Armageddon is upon us! Why don't one of you *say* something for God's sake!" says Ken.

"Got any smokes?" Gladys asks.

❧

THE PATIENTS ARE UPSET. Gladys, who's usually happy, is upset. She has been sneaking out to the patio waiting to be snatched away. Trying to reason with her is useless; she'll only start yelling and flapping her hands: "I DID SO MEET THE LORD. DID SO! AND I DON'T WANT ANY MORE APPLES EITHER!"

The entire ward has discussed nothing but rapture and the bombing of Baghdad. Things have gotten out of hand. Harold sees blood on people's faces. He hears voices calling Ken Satan. Gladys has taken to smoking for hours on the patio. Given her increasing agitation, Dr. Cooper is afraid she might burn the place down.

Patients are complaining they're depressed, getting worse, not better. "We don't need religion," they say, "What we want is therapy!" Ken, however, is not depressed at all. On the contrary: "What a way to live! A new dawn!" he constantly exclaims.

The doctor thinks Ken's attitude is improving. To counteract what he calls "nuclear war phobias" Dr. Cooper has taken away Harold's radio. He has prohibited the patients from watching the news. Now Dr. Cooper is proposing they put Gladys on a behaviour modification program to reduce her smoking. "We could ration her cigarettes, teach her more socially useful behavior," he says.

When Ellie hears this, she is outraged. "Sure Gladys is a bit jittery. Who isn't?" she says. "Ken's got everyone thinking the world's coming to an end. Have you heard him?" Ellie raises her arms in the air in imitation and calls out loudly: "True Christians need not fear. Indeed, we have the hope of Christ's return and our being joined to Him forever!"

Dr. Cooper shrugs. "He's a born-again Christian."

"No," Ellie says, "he's a deranged, dangerous man."

"Just because you don't happen to agree with him?" the doctor laughs.

"No. But you call someone who prays for the end of the world healthy?"

Dr. Cooper shakes his head. "Actually, Ellie, it's not that simple, as any expert on phobias will tell you. Now we can take away Harold's radio. We can limit Gladys's cigarettes. We can stop the patients from watching the news. But I'm sure you'll agree that won't solve their problems. Maybe," he says, "it's time for Ken to develop a relationship with another nurse."

DR. COOPER APPOINTS a tall blonde named Liz. Ken likes Liz. Liz with her smart look, her stylish dresses and high heels. Liz wouldn't oppose him. Liz doesn't tell him he won't rapture. "Tall, dark and handsome. He's rather good-looking," Liz tells Ellie, "Don't you think?" Sitting in the day room next to Liz, Ellie, who on principle dresses casually so as not to set herself apart from the patients, ends up looking like one of them.

Ken has said to Liz in "strictest confidence" that he would never have laid a hand on his wife were it not for his relationship with Suzette, their ten-year-old daughter.

When Liz asks, "What *was* your relationship with Suzette?" Ken winks and won't say anything. Liz wants to write "suspected molesting" on his chart but Dr. Cooper has asked her not to. A chart's a legal document that can be subpoenaed in court, Liz says, and Dr. Cooper's afraid they'll be sued.

Ellie is incredulous. "If Ken told anything of the sort to me," she says, "I'd chart it no matter what."

"Chart *what*, exactly?" says Liz. "None of us knows what Ken did."

Ellie says she can guess.

"Me too," says Liz. "But I think he's having regrets."

NOW KEN SAUNTERS around the ward, winking at Liz constantly. Ellie is certain he's told Liz *exactly* what he did to Suzette.

"I like being his confidante. You know, he's quite an interesting guy, and not at all crazy once you get to know him," Liz says.

"Precisely right," Ellie answers, "he's not crazy at all, he knows exactly what he's doing. Write it down."

"PILL-TIME!" ELLIE CALLS into the day room.

"Well, and what do we have here today?" Ken says, as he lifts a Lily cup off her tray.

"Something for Gladys," says Ellie impatiently. "Give it back, Ken."

Ken opens his yellow satchel. In go Gladys's antidepressants. Out comes a yo-yo. "Want to see me walk the dog?" he says.

The yo-yo walks across the floor toward Gladys.

"How about 'round the world'?"

He swings the yo-yo past Gladys's ear.

Ellie puts down the tray and reaches for the satchel. Ken holds it high above his head.

"Ken, I want those pills."

His eyes roam over her blouse. "Are you supposed to be a nurse? You don't have tits like a nurse."

The yo-yo whizzes past her.

"Give me those pills or I'll call an orderly."

"Now that's not nice. You're supposed to be nice to me." He comes up close, his warm breath right in her face. The kaftan drapes open. He gives her a superior smile. "You know, if we take the case of Jesus . . . . Jesus could have gotten off if he'd had me for a lawyer."

Ellie backs away.

"Yes," he says loudly, as he comes toward her, "you've got to be Jesus to get out of here. Or a lawyer." He winks at Gladys. "Eh, Ellie, eh?"

Ellie goes to get an orderly.

"Okay then, *crucify me!*"

Ken throws down the satchel. He flings his arms up and out to the side. The yo-yo dangles.

IT IS A SUNNY DAY—the day Saddam Hussein, trying to rally his fledging troops, pledges peace—when Ken leaves the psych ward to catch his plane to Calgary, waving happily. He gives Liz a kiss goodbye. "Thanks, honey, I've had such a good time," he says. He looks around the day room and when he doesn't see Ellie, adds loudly, "Will you be sure to give Ellie my love too?"

"Come on," says Dr. Cooper, holding Ken's suitcase as they leave for the airport in Dr. Cooper's air-conditioned BMW.

Ellie pictures Ken's plane flying high, high above the clouds. She imagines him looking down from his window seat, musing contentedly. How the water sparkles like diamonds! What perfection below! Ellie can hear him chatting with a woman in the next seat, telling her all about the psych ward.

"Oh no, it's not what you think." Maybe he laughs, just a little. "I wasn't a patient, I'm a lawyer, I consulted on a case." Then, bending close, lowering his voice: "An abuse case, actually."

Does the woman believe him? Ellie wonders. Of course she believes him. Ellie pictures the woman looking up, startled as she remarks only too innocently, "Horrible, isn't it, what a person can get away with these days."

"Well, some of my clients do say the girls led them on," Ken says.

And the woman answers: "Of course, that's what they'd say."

"Who knows?" Here, there's a pause. Ken's in no rush, no hurry at all. Why get excited? He boasts of a life-time studying cases. "Why, I even defended a man who said his five-year-old daughter wouldn't leave him alone, not for a minute. Followed him right into the bathtub," Ken says. "So what do you do in a case like that?"

"Don't believe it. Not a word of it," says the woman, shaking her head.

Ken shrugs. "Well, you must have heard of that recent case—the three-year-old who the judge said was sexually precocious . . . ."

Suddenly there's a loud engine noise. The stewardess' voice comes over the loudspeaker telling everyone to remain calm. Ken clutches his seat. The woman next to him begins to pray. "Oh for God's sake," says Ken, "if you think that's going to help any . . . ." Ellie sees him raise his eyes to heaven.

ELLIE AND LIZ HEAR the details at work the following day. The plane hit a mountainside and scraped along the trees. People were thrown out. Several reported still missing.

"Think he made it?" Ellie asks.

"Who knows?" Liz says. "Remember what he used to say?"

"You don't believe that 'wafting up' stuff, do you?" Ellie laughs.

"Well," says Liz, "Ken never did want to take that plane."

Lunch comes. Reports pour forth from the TV room. News of the victory in the Gulf. Parades and yellow ribbons. Clips from a military-produced rock video: throbbing crescendos as laser-guided bombs make contact with their targets. The patients are afraid to leave the room and eat. What if they miss something?

Evening comes. A life-size Mickey Mouse dances with U.S. Commanding General "Stormin' Norman". No one wants to go to sleep.

SEVERAL DAYS LATER, Ellie receives a Jesus calling card.

Think of me when you look out your window at night. I'll be in touch.

On Harold's radio, the coverage continues, the mood celebratory, exultant. No one talks of death. "What is it like for you in Tel Aviv? Dhahran? Riyadh? *How do you feel?*" the "Talk Back" show host asks again and again. "*Now that it's all over, how do you feel? How do you feel?*"

Les Amants

EVEN BEFORE SHE OPENED the envelope, Louisa knew something was wrong. In place of a return address there were only initials. Then, inside, the pages were scrambled. Page one left off half-way down the middle; it picked up on page three, while on the second page there was only a short paragraph at the top. It began with *Here I am, looking at hummingbirds,* and went on to describe a bird sanctuary André had gone to. He noted the birds that came into his view. The sounds seagulls made. The way a great blue heron stood, motionless, balanced on one leg. When she saw the word *balanced,* Louisa remembered going up a steep winding path which led through the woods. Stopping, André had turned to her. He told her he had never been in love like this. He looked at her for some time, then said, "I want to remember this moment." He believed memories were indelibly held in the body, that if he kissed her then, she would hold him forever beneath her skin. "This is so real. So real I can't believe it," he told her. And now, six months later, he was using the same words about someone else.

THE OTHER WOMAN—Marilyn—was an artist's model. André painted women. He painted semi-nudes in Art Nouveau style. He and Louisa had met at the opening of his one-man exhibit in the local gallery.

Louisa's favourite painting, *The Flowers and Fruit*, featured a spectacular blonde wreathed in brilliant red poppies and bearing an armful of apples. What had caught her eye at the exhibit was the woman's expression. She couldn't be sure whether the subject was being celebrated or mocked. When André walked over to her and she asked him about his intention, he shrugged with a laugh. "But that's up to you."

He had a generous laugh which resonated from inside. It gave Louisa a feeling of comfort, of being with someone familiar. Yet she was equally aware of his mystery. She found his boyish looks, the brown leather jacket he wore open, his hair falling over one eye, appealing, exciting.

"The poppies are so lush, I could eat them!" she said.

They began to discuss her marriage, her three children. He said he was the father of two and divorced. He would be in town for a few days and wondered if Louisa would like to show him around.

That afternoon, going for a walk in the park, André talked about why his wife had left him. She found his need for solitude too much to bear. Her own marriage, Louisa described as nearly perfect.

Hearing herself boast, Louisa blushed.

"Come on, every marriage has its flaws," André laughed.

Louisa shrugged. She wished Martin worked less; a geologist, he often spent weeks out in the field. "Still, I'm happy. Very happy," she said. "The only thing is, sometimes when I think I may never paint again . . . ."

André stopped and looked at her. "Nobody else can paint what you see. That's why you keep doing it."

Simple words, but gracious, kind. They gave her courage. Full of gratitude, she pulled André close. She had the sensation of falling into him, feeling everything in her break open. How long had it been since a man held her like that? When they came away from each other, she said, "I thought we were just walking and talking. I can't explain."

"Then don't," André told her.

"But I hardly know you. We just met."

He laughed. "You're so serious. Are you always this serious?" He smoothed back her hair.

"But how can I feel this way? I don't know what to do."

He shrugged, still laughing. "We can always say goodbye."

OVER THE MONTHS, André had often referred to Marilyn, the model, in passing, though not in entirely complimentary terms. Once he told her that Marilyn was not as courageous as she. "You don't realize how much your bravery means to me," he said.

Louisa told him she envied Marilyn, sharing his studio and working alongside him, a free agent, while she was married and lived so far away.

He said, "But she's not free. Look at the walls she puts up around her."

He also talked about his ex-wife. She had been a wonderful mother to their two children. He knew she would be, he said, it was the reason he'd married her. But what else did she do with herself?

Louisa told him she thought that was uncalled for, especially when he'd been married to her for twelve years. It made her feel like phoning up his wife and having a talk.

"What about?" he said.

"You, of course."

"Me?"

She pictured his smile. He liked being the centre of things.

She began to imagine herself trying to get free of him, but was always frozen in place. She often had dreams of paralysis—one of the children, usually her youngest, might be hurt but she would be unable to reach him. She could hear him calling, "Mommy, mommy, where are you?" but she could not make herself move. She knew the dream had nothing to do with reality. Still, she went into the children's rooms every hour. Later, laughing, she would tell Martin, "After all is said and done, what else am I but a mother?" The words had a calming effect. She was a good mother. Though people asked about her 'other life' ("How's my favourite painter?" "Still teaching art classes?") her real role, she felt, was to care for her children.

❧

ANDRÉ SAID SHE FELT GUILT, a guilt he thought unnecessary.

Now she remembered the way he'd looked at her in the hotel bath, as a young girl, her hair flowing above her breasts in the water. She remembered telling herself, *I don't know, it just sort of happened.* How could something like that happen to her? Was it sordid? There had to be a reason—at the very least, a bad marriage. But her marriage was not bad, and here she was.

Days later when he'd phoned from the city to say his plane had landed safely, Louisa told him, told him straight-out in what she liked to think of as that no-nonsense way of hers, "I'm in love with you, and I don't know how to handle it."

"But the idea always is to love *yourself,* Louisa," he said. "Our embrace in the park—don't you remember? You surrendered. Not to me, to yourself. That's what we're trying to do, isn't it? That's where the struggle is."

"Struggle? What struggle? Don't you understand? I just told you I'm in love with you! It's fine for you to talk about me loving myself," she protested, "but what about my *marriage?* Do you care about what happens to Martin and me? I'm not saying I don't want you in my life. Of course I do. I want you as an additional pleasure, not a replacement for what I have."

Guilt. Unnecessary guilt, he told her. "Guilt is not even a real emotion," he said. They had slept together only once; sheer distance made future trysts unlikely. Besides, both had been clear with each other, knew what they *didn't* want—the break-up of her marriage—from the start. She loved her husband. Indeed, hadn't she said she loved Martin now more than ever *because* of what had happened? That she felt renewed commitment, passion? Things had gone well; why blame herself needlessly?

All this he told her late at night while her children slept, her husband away, the house so cold Louisa shivered. She couldn't get the gas heater to work. Martin hadn't turned on the switch in the basement.

Then, one night several weeks ago when Louisa phoned, she got an answering machine. An impersonal voice, "You've reached . . ." and a searing beep. She tried again the next night. On the third night she left her name, with a curt message, "Please phone back."

He phoned at midnight. "Your voice on the machine . . . . Is anything the matter?"

"Oh no. Only that I wondered where you were. Whether you were all right," she said.

"You're sure? Your kids?"

"No, no," she assured him, somewhat embarrassed. "Nothing like that."

"Then what is it, Louisa?"

The question—was it the tone of his voice? A sudden

impatience perhaps? Was someone in the room with him?

"You know I love ya kid," he laughed.

COMPARED TO ANDRÉ'S OTHER LETTERS, the one from the bird sanctuary was neater, the impression the type-written words made, precise, sharp. *Writing letters is actually an intercourse with ghosts,* he wrote her, *and by no means just with the ghost of the addressee but also with one's own ghost, which secretly evolves inside the letter* . . . .

He said it was a line he'd come across in a letter Kafka wrote Milena Jesenská with whom he was in love for most of his life. *I've been thinking about this in relation to us,* André wrote.

Other letters had been written by hand in flowing purple or magenta ink.

After they separated and he returned to the city, he had gone alone to the mountains. The moon rose and he realized he was being led somewhere by forces he could not see. *Have you ever had that kind of feeling?* he wrote her. *Have you ever felt that something was so right you would venture without knowing where you were going, without asking questions?*

Dear A, she wrote back, *Is a platonic relationship between a man and woman who have slept together really possible? Is it okay if I think of you touching my breast?*

How about a different kind of love story? he asked. *How about a story where two people come to love each other without joining?*

He seemed so open to her, so committed to friendship, that Louisa felt awkward, foolish for the turmoil of emotions their connection aroused.

Dear A, she replied, *I think about you constantly, too much. I feel consumed.*

That evening, putting the children to bed, a curious image formed in her mind.

Dear A, I'm painting again! It's an abstract piece with a flash of red. I see your face. I feel sixteen again.

He phoned three days later. Could she come to Vancouver and spend a few days with him?

She laughed. "You're joking."

"Louisa, is there something wrong with two painters—*artistes*—getting together? I'm sure Martin would understand."

"And who would take care of the kids?"

"Why Martin, of course."

She laughed again. Had he gone crazy? she asked. Absolutely lost his mind?

Later, while Martin lay sleeping beside her, she began to wonder. What if she and Martin weren't in love any more? What if they were just adjusted to the *idea?* What if, after all, they were simply good friends who stayed together because they loved their children, and there didn't seem to be any reason to part?

She got out of bed, went downstairs and rummaged through her postcards.

Dear A, Dear A, she wrote on the back of Picasso's *Les Amants. There are so many beginnings and they each lead somewhere else. I'm in love with you, but I think I hardly know you.*

PHONE SEX.

The first time, it happened by chance. She was simply describing some clothes she had bought. How she had gone idly from one shop to another trying them on. Black sequined sweaters, leopard-skin leggings, silk camisoles and garter belts . . . . She began imagining him taking her clothes off.

"Do you really want me to be telling you this?" Louisa laughed self-consciously. Martin always said he liked her best in her old flannel paint shirt with its tattered collar and sleeves.

"Hmmm, I don't know," André said. "Do you want to tell me?"

His voice, deep and melodic, mesmerized her. She waited, transfixed. But why not go on? It was one in the morning; neither could get to sleep.

SOMETIMES LOUISA PLOTTED to forget him. He was a womanizer; why else did he paint those ornate semi-nudes with their ambiguous expressions?

She had burned all her love letters before marrying Martin, erased the past. Now she wondered: what about André's letters?

At night, making love with her husband, when she thought of the phone calls with André, she would tell herself, *It's only fantasy. People fantasize all the time.* Tell herself as she straddled Martin with a new found passion, *It's all in my head anyway,* and he, exhausted after working long hours, laughed, delighted.

The truth was, they had not made love like this in

years, not since the children were born. Did he ever wonder? she asked herself.

Sometimes when she talked about André, Louisa was sure her husband could sense her deception.

"André phoned today," she would say.

"Oh? And how's he doing?"

"Okay. Sold a few paintings. Says he might come for another exhibit at the gallery."

"Already—so soon?"

"Well, it's been several months."

He would look at her then with an uncertain look that made her heart cry out.

"Martin, is anything the matter?"

HE WAS LOOKING AT HER NOW.

She was so immersed in the letter she had not heard his key in the door. She had not heard him come in.

He was looking at her, touching her cheeks moist with tears, saying, "Louisa, Louisa, what's wrong?"

He was looking at her as he took her by the hand. Looking at her as he led her to the couch and sat down beside her.

It was late, the children asleep, the house dark and quiet as Louisa pressed her body against his, wrapped Martin in her arms and held him tightly. But as he touched her, comforted her, looked at her, her lover's voice whispered: *Don't go yet. I've got something to tell you. I'm writing you a letter. . . .*

Lovers and Other Strangers

I READ A STORY TODAY about a woman who gets paid five thousand bucks by a complete stranger for a cool fuck. At least, "cool fuck" were his words. I was frankly surprised, but then what do I know about writers?

When I met him that day and asked what he was doing, he replied: "Give me your hand." I did, obediently, and turning it over he traced his fingers along the palm. "I read lines," he said. I had trouble even then believing him. He wore sunglasses.

First, I can't help but correct a few minor details: my bathing suit was green, not yellow; the beach was

Taghum, not Turtle Cove; and though it's true that I have a tattoo on my upper arm, it is not a pair of flying hearts as he says but a butterfly. I told him that the Spanish for butterfly is *mariposa*—my childhood nickname. Though I don't recall him ever calling me that.

We ate at the Mews, not the Downtowner. He had one of his usual bland omelettes; I, a hot Szechwan tofu. Later we went to my apartment and talked about our first marriages. It's true that when he laughed at my "naiveté" I told him to watch out, that I might just fall in love with him. But I certainly never said that coming with him was like "staring into God's eyes," and (perhaps the most important for reasons which I'll later discuss) I did not use Vaseline. I never use Vaseline. Not since my mother told me in 1964, when I was fourteen years old, that Vaseline is a gasoline by-product. "Petroleum product" is, in fact, what it says on the jar. So not Vaseline. Not then, not ever.

I must say he does seem quite insistent on having the last word: "Flat." After re-reading the final paragraphs of the story, I still don't understand. I get this far: the woman is fucked from behind ("doggy-style" he says in the story), after coating herself with Vaseline, from *his* bathroom. He comes quickly. ("Don't worry about that," he says, "I always come quick the first time.")

He turns away from her with a low moan: "Oh God!" She asks for the money, and he says it's in the other room. She tells him to put on his clothes first. He goes into the other room, naked, returns in a robe (a maroon robe, he says; probably the only correct detail) and hands her the envelope. She opens it: five thousand in cash. "I thought cash would be better," he says, "in case you had difficulty with a cheque." By this time she's already put on her clothes (a green, not yellow bathing suit), has picked up her canvas bag (really a blue knapsack) and is about to walk out the door. That's when she turns to him and says, "Can we do this again, sometime?" And he looks at her steel grey eyes that (he incorrectly presumes) resemble her father's. "No, you've been had," he says. "Flat."

Tell me, what does the word *flat* mean? He's already mentioned her "shapely figure," and surely he's not alluding to the sexual positioning. Something to do with their conversation perhaps? Dull, insubstantial, humourless? I think not, especially when he admits to his wanting (insisting, in fact on) their "sparse interchange."

Perhaps *flat* refers, then, to their culinary dispositions: her taste for spicy Indonesian foods; his, for bland Western dishes. Or the fact that she sips on her Coke while he downs one Rum Collins after another. He does compare her occasional desire for a Coke to his equally occasional desire for a cool fuck. "When you want a Coke you just go out and buy it," he tells her. "But a Coke doesn't cost five thousand dollars!" she protests. He tosses her a magazine lying on the glass coffee table. "Read the recent interview with me on Wall Street." She looks at him inquisitively. "The money means nothing to me," he explains.

He's so convincing in print, like a magician who puts the lady in a box and right before our eyes saws her into two, later revealing that she's all in one piece. How easily we are fooled. What cunning, what sleight of hand kept me reading on, past "moist cunt" and "hot wench," feeling myself getting physically excited as the shopkeeper (a short balding man with horn-rimmed glasses) kept walking past me to re-fill his candy rack and shelve new magazines. "Why do you sell such trash!" I wanted to scream. He had me till the very end.

But the five thousand dollars? Evidently he's forgotten.

He couldn't take the bus. He wouldn't have made it to his next reading. Instead, he borrowed five hundred dollars and bought a ticket for the plane.

IN THE BEGINNING (it seems only proper to start there, after all) our encounter was quite simple and ordinary. We met on the beach at Taghum and it was very hot. I was sunning myself in my green nylon tank suit, reading a best-seller by Atwood. I suppose—my pen and paper by my feet—he suspected I was literary.

I felt something dark and cold come over me, as he blocked the sun.

"Can I join you?" he said, more a statement than question.

"Of course."

He sat down on my plaid flannel car blanket, at a respectable distance. He wore sunglasses.

"What are you reading?" he asked.

"Lady Oracle."

"One of my favourites. I like the way she disappears, just when you think you know her," he said.

"What are you doing here?" I asked, trying not to appear too negative or critical.

He ordered me to give him my hand and when I did—star-struck? dazed?—he turned it over, palms up.

"I read lines," he said.

"Oh, you're an actor."

"No, a writer," he replied, his sharp white teeth showing through his thin lips.

I still couldn't see his eyes.

LATER, IN THE MEWS, he told me he was a stranger in town and would be catching a bus in a week, that he'd been on the road giving readings.

"So, now that I've told you my all," he challenged, "what have you heard about me?"

I traced my finger gently across his lips. "I like you. I want to trust my senses," I said.

I felt beautiful; brave, glorious, enchanting. He was wearing a heather green sweater which heightened the grey colour of his eyes. He looked away and then back at me. He cracked a joke, made it all seem light, funny, which it was not.

A FEW DAYS LATER we drove to Gyro Park. He held my hand a long time. Finally, he told me how difficult he found it to be forward with women.

I laughed and kissed him lightly. "That's what I like about you."

"No, you don't understand, I've never been the kind of man women wanted."

I put his hand to my mouth and licked his fingers.

"I love making love to you. You're beautiful," I said.

"Sex is only one room. Only one aspect."

"Oh? Why so down? I think you're afraid to be happy." I laughed.

"I guess if I were I'd have nothing to write about."

I couldn't dispel his fears, not being a writer myself. But I wanted to tell him as one fellow-traveller to another that happiness and creativity are not incompatible. "Look at me," I said. "I've managed to become a skilled potter and I'm happy."

"Throwing a pot is not like writing a novel," he asserted.

"Why not?"

"Words are invisible. Invisibility is what gives words their power."

I smiled at his sobriety. "I don't understand what we're arguing about. I can't control what happens, and neither can you. We just have to trust each other," I whispered.

"Who's *we?*" he said.

I thought it was obvious.

THAT WEEK WE SPENT TOGETHER we made love constantly in my apartment overlooking the lake. His bus came and went. We barely went outside, barely ate anything. If at all, it was something tart, something with our fingers.

I've often thought of sending him a pineapple with a playful note: *Come, for a visit.* I can still feel the sweet wet taste of the fruit when I kissed him.

I kissed him all over, breathed pineapple through the pores of his skin.

Satellite Worlds

each thought conjures demons
every word invites trouble
—*THE MOUNTAIN POEMS OF STONEHOUSE*

JUST BEFORE DENISE'S HUSBAND LEFT HER for another woman, Denise asked, "What's she got that I don't have?"

"Something new and exciting," Norm said.

Needless to say, Norm and his "something new and exciting" didn't last too long, but Denise never forgave Norm, nor did she ever forget.

"So, what's new and exciting in your life now?" she asked whenever he came to pick up the kids.

Norm flashed the kids a teasing smile and said, "Your mom's lookin' real good," but Denise guessed he wasn't happy. It wasn't as if their relationship had been bad. Much of their eight years as a couple they'd spent apart. Norm's work took him north to consult on the effects of PCBs on polar bears. Denise, a freelance journalist who hoped someday to break into fiction, had mothered their children. Each time Norm returned from a trip it had taken her awhile to get used to him, but she looked forward to that. Candles. Incense. Wine. Her soft sand-washed silk negligée, the rose satin sheets.

She'd met Norm through a personal ad: *Libra male, early 40s, tall, dark and . . . well, acceptably attractive, enjoys living in the country. Into gourmet foods, candle-light dinners. Loves garlic, adventure. Looking for independent, self-starting woman, 30–35, for some adventure close to home.*

Denise had been sceptical—nearly everyone she knew was using some dating service—but she fell for Norm instantly. They met in a "Rare and Used" bookstore.

Denise began the first page of her novel. The man's name would be Colin . . . .

> *When they met, quite accidentally in the lobby of a video dating service, Colin seemed rather shy. He said he'd been just about to quit the dating service when Désirée, a tall blonde in a white dress exposing her deeply tanned body, came into the lobby.*

Wrong. All wrong. She didn't tan; she burned.
In the bookstore, Norm had approached cautiously.
"Are you Denise?"

Denise nodded. His eyes opened wide. Jet black eyes, taking her in . . . .

> That night in Désirée's apartment, Colin told her about the women he had been with. He confessed to having made mistakes with them. Then he spoke about X: "I'll call her that. I can't tell you her name." X had six orgasms a night, each quite powerful.

Six orgasms? Is that possible? Denise stopped writing to consider. Perhaps she should do an informal survey?

> "My first two video dates were controlling women," Colin went on. "Though you wouldn't have known from their videos."
>
> Each person made a video answering questions about preferences. Colin was in the dating service lobby when X, wearing only a black sundress and white sandals, came in.
>
> "Imagine my surprise," Colin said, "when she asked for a ride home."
>
> The walls of X's kitchen were covered with pho-tographs of women's breasts. Her living room had a piano so large you had to crawl under or step around it. Colin pressed her onto the bench; X pulled up the sundress . . . . Later, they made love standing up in her hallway, X being too aroused, he said, to reach the bedroom.

Denise looked up from what she had written, pleased—early experience as a writer having led her to believe that someone must always be either making love or getting killed.

It was Norm's view that men told you everything you needed to know about them in the first five minutes. "They warn you about themselves," Norm had told her.

Denise tried to remember: what *had* Norm said, leaving the bookstore? That he liked traveling. That he wasn't sure he liked being in love.

"Seriously. I don't do relationships well," Norm, nursing a beer in her kitchen, admitted.

Then Norm told her how there were probably eight or nine women in the world who wanted nothing to do with him.

He said, "In the past I've loved ruthlessly."

Ruthlessly? Denise laughed. "Isn't that a bit melodramatic?"

"I've been told I'm the secretive type, but I think I've been honest with them."

"Ah, but secrets are where the gold is!" Denise said. "Tell me a secret of yours. Just one."

But he wouldn't.

"I don't mean to pry," she said one evening, years later. "But I get the feeling you're harbouring, not sharing, the gold."

By their eighth year together, she felt desperate. It was no longer Norm's secretiveness that bothered Denise; it was her own.

"That night you were in Yellowknife," she began, "when it was twenty-five below . . . ?"

"Yes?" Norm looked at her.

"I slept with someone."

"Well then, I guess we're even!" Norm threw his head back and laughed.

"You mean you slept with someone too?" Denise asked. She felt relieved, though his response admittedly wasn't what she'd been expecting. "So," she teased lightly, "what's she got that I don't have?"

The affair had been going on for a year.

When Colin told her about X (he still refused to use her name), Désirée was furious. It wasn't only the fact that he said they'd made love standing up in X's hallway, but the way he took a certain pleasure in elaborating on the details. The grand piano. The breasts in the kitchen. The ornate wallpaper in the hall.

"X believes you need to express all parts of yourself," Colin said, "even those you may not like or understand."

"And what parts are those?" Désirée asked.

"The dark side," Colin enunciated in his faint British accent. "In the end, I suppose that's what I'll always remember about her, what I really liked."

She laughed. "Apart from the great sex."

"No, you're getting it all wrong. Deep down, X was really a Victorian! She was so embarrassed about it that instead of telling anyone she'd bought herself this beautiful old-fashioned four-poster bed."

"Why?" Désirée said. "She certainly didn't use it."

Denise pictured Norm's smile as she put down her pen. "Oh the power of the mind!" he'd told her. "Out of nothing it creates oceans."

Norm was a meditator. Before they'd met, he'd been in a car accident and had to spend several months flat on his back. He couldn't even read then, the pain was so excruciating, he said. "I had a traffic counter—a push button affair—and just lay on my back repeating over and over, 'I can enjoy the present moment.' CLICK. 'I can enjoy the present moment.' CLICK. 'I can enjoy the present moment . . . .'"

Everything had a purpose—even suffering, he told her. "You must never let go of suffering too soon—even though the seeking mind *drives* you to go beyond it, you musn't. Suffering shows you the truth."

"My passion is the truth," Denise said. "I'd go to any length to find it."

DENISE'S BOOK WAS NOT GOING WELL. True, the title, *Satellite Worlds*, had a nice ring—if only she could find its relevance. Twin suns? Each the centre of the other's orbit? With Zack home from kindergarten at noon, and Katie, two years older, catching one thing after another—chicken pox, head lice, the flu—how could she accomplish anything?

Saturday morning, though as a rule Denise never wrote on weekends, she put the children in front of a video, closed her study door and sat down at her desk.

"So," said Colin playfully, "do you have any favourite fantasies? Come on, let me interview you, video style. Is there anything you wouldn't do? Think. S and M? Bondage?"

"I'm afraid I don't have much imagination,"
Désirée said.

"Does this help?" He placed his hand on her
breast.

"Colin, stop." Désirée gasped. The photographs
on X's walls stared at her: pointed breasts, pendu-
lous breasts, breasts large and small. "Don't you
know how impossible you are?"

"Impossible? Who's impossible?"

Again he reached for her. He was reaching for her
over the coffee table. He overturned a teacup. A
plate of cookies fell to the floor. "I'd like to see you
come … your face at the moment of orgasm!" he
cried. When he went to kiss her, he put a finger
inside her mouth.

"Zack, what do you think Mommy writes about anyway?"

"Dad says she writes about gross stuff."

The children were blowing whistles. They had turned
on the stereo and were dancing. They were beating
drums.

Denise tried to get back to her writing. She pictured
Colin bending over Désirée. He was stroking her ten-
derly. They were naked, making love on the floor—

Suddenly there was a loud crash. Wailing.

"Mom, Mom! Zack just fell and cut his lip!"

Denise yanked the door open. "JUST FOR ONCE
CAN'T YOU LEAVE ME ALONE!"

She apologized, the children apologized, she bandaged
Zack's lip. "Now how about you two playing outside? I
can watch you from the living room."

Once they'd gone, Denise stood by the window watching them—building mounds, digging holes, piling stones. She unplugged the phone, organized her desk and sat down to write. But the words wouldn't come. They would not come. Her head ached. There was a dull pain in her chest.

And now, dammit, the doorbell. The kids were playing with the doorbell.

Denise glanced at her watch—nearly a half hour. Probably the children were bored. Or hungry. Or had to go to the bathroom. Not that it mattered; she couldn't write. In a few hours Norm would come to take them.

Denise went to the door. She hadn't realized it was locked.

"Mom, come quick! Zack's on the roof! He's frightened and won't come down."

Katie started to cry. Denise ran past her into the yard. Sure enough, he'd gotten up on the roof outside his bedroom. Norm's ladder, the one for cherry picking, was propped against the house.

"Zack—honey? It's gonna be all right, just stay where you are." Denise tried to keep her voice calm.

Katie sobbed. "Why *won't* Zack come down?" She held onto Denise's waist tightly. "We were having so much fun up there, looking at the mountains."

"You were on the roof too?" Denise sighed, loudly. "How many times have I told you—"

"Mom, please." Katie looked at her imploringly. The woman next door had come into the yard.

"We tried phoning." The woman looked pointedly at Denise.

"Oh my God." Mortified, Denise apologized.

"Katie said the phone might be unplugged. That I shouldn't disturb you, you were writing. I knocked on your door but I guess you didn't hear. We finally got hold of Norm through his mother." The neighbour turned around. "Isn't that his truck pulling in?"

Denise looked. Norm was walking down the driveway. Katie ran to him, pulling him by the arm. "Daddy, Daddy."

Norm glanced up. "Don't worry, son. Daddy's here to take care of you. Denise, you could at least unlatch his window."

Minutes later, Zack safe in his arms, Norm glared. "So, you were writing today, while your children were on the roof. And the neighbours trying to phone."

His voice was contemptuous. He stared at her.

"Look at you. Eleven a.m. You're not even dressed."

"Norm, I don't think—"

"*Think?* How do you think I feel having the neighbours call my mother because you're sitting in the house writing and won't answer your goddamm phone? What kind of mother are you?"

"Norm, please." Denise looked at her children. Katie clung to his arm; Zack, to his neck. Why didn't they let go of him? In a moment he would explode at her. She could see it coming. He would rally all the amunition. Her housekeeping. Her cooking. She was always in her head. There was no use in saying he never paid child support or that he took the kids only once a month. He would claim all she ever thought about was herself. That's why he'd left her.

"So," Norm said, "did the kids get their breakfast?"

"What?"

"Are you feeding them properly?"

"Norm, really—" She laughed.

"Oh and by the way, since you're not doing anything, think you can put the ladder away? It belongs in the garage."

❧

THAT AFTERNOON SHE SAT at the computer with a box of Ritz Mini Bits. Occasionally, when there was a break in her thoughts, Denise would nibble a cracker. By Sunday night, when Norm returned with the kids, she had written well over one hundred pages and handed him a copy.

"My book."

"You want me to read it?" Norm said, incredulous.

"Yes, I do," Denise said. She wasn't sure why. Norm had often joked about what a lousy journalist she made—always getting involved with her stories, writing in the first person.

She wanted to tell him simply, "This happened."

Of course he wouldn't believe her.

That was the thing about fiction.

❧

HE CALLED A WEEK LATER from a phone booth up north. It was cold, thirty below; he couldn't talk long, he said, he had a touch of the flu. "I can tell you're beginning to trust yourself. I knew you had it in you," he told her. "You know how I've always loved your mind." He sounded out of breath. Surprised.

"So, you really liked it?"

"Yes . . . well . . . ." Norm hesitated.

"You know," Denise explained, "sometimes I feel so exiled, as if I'm standing outside the gates of Eden. No moment is pure, nothing is immune."

"So, I can tell you what I really think? You won't mind?"

"Not at all."

"Well, if that's how you feel . . . . I do find some of it unbelievable," Norm said.

"But it all happened, it's all true," said Denise. "One way or another."

"Maybe. But what you wrote about X . . . ?" There was a pause. "Denise, we didn't make love standing up in her hallway."

"Of course," said Denise happily, "you know how writers invent."

"Though you're right about one thing. You won't be angry if I tell you?"

"Of course not."

"You're sure?"

"It'll be very helpful."

"We didn't use her bed. We made love outside," Norm said.

"Outside? In thirty below?"

"She had a tent."

"Oh, I see," said Denise, opening her notebook, jotting down: *flu, 30 below, tent.*

"She had this thing about being outside," Norm said. "Her tent had this transparent material—you know, sewn in at the top? You could see the stars."

"I see, I see," said Denise, writing.